What did I know about the seventh man? I opened a beer and sat back.

The seventh man had unlimited money and information.

The seventh man knew that Al had protested. And Al had died.

The seventh man had warned me to lay off. As a further inducement, he had shot at me.

My mind burned with red heat, because I wanted my own hands to have a part in shaping the end of the seventh man. It was becoming more and more impossible for me to pull out.

I knew death might be at the end of the road. But I was going down that road, and waiting at the end would be

THE SEVENTH MAN

By America's Master Storyteller

JOHN JAKES

ATTENTION: SCHOOLS AND CORPORATIONS

PINNACLE Books are available at quantity discounts with bulk purchases for educational, business or special promotional use. For further details, please write to: SPECIAL SALES MANAGER, Pinnacle Books, Inc., 1430 Broadway, New York, NY 10018.

WRITE FOR OUR FREE CATALOG

If there is a Pinnacle Book you want—and you cannot find it locally—it is available from us simply by sending the title and price plus 75¢ to cover mailing and handling costs to:

Pinnacle Books, Inc.
Reader Service Department
1430 Broadway
New York, NY 10018

Please allow 6 weeks for delivery.

_____Check here if you want to receive our catalog regularly.

JOHN JAKES

THE SEVENTH MAN

TOR

A TOM DOHERTY ASSOCIATES BOOK

Distributed by Pinnacle Books, New York

THE SEVENTH MAN

Copyright © 1958 by Thomas Bouregy & Company

A Tor Book

First printing, October 1981

ISBN: 0-523-48018-0

Cover illustration by Bruce Minney

Printed in the United States of America

Distributed by Pinnacle Books, 1430 Broadway, New York, N.Y. 10018

TO

John Damon
*and a friendship begun to the
sound of
Purple Parrots.*

CHAPTER I

At ten o'clock of a sweltering August night I sat in my two-by-four office staring at my Royal, its roller like a black bar of accusation across my eyes. My shirt was plastered to my body and I was tired. But it was mostly the heat—the smothering, sticky-wet heat of a Chicago summer. Somewhere in the heart of this tall building my friends were readying the Late City edition, rewriting and jerking· stuff that had died since the Eight-O'clock had hit the stands, changing heads, make-up, switching break-overs, doing a thousand other things. All of them busy, all of them fine examples of the Working Press at work. All but me, Harry Diamond, as I sat hunched over my machine, not a wheel turning, any semblance of an idea for my column, "Personally Speaking," stillborn from this breathless heat.

Right now, I told myself, I was letting down my readers who—so I fondly hoped—were looking forward to my thousand words of breezy gossip and news from the local night spots, hotels, and Rialto circuit. With a rapidly melting hour to get my stuff wrapped up and into the copy desk, my alleged brain was as blank as the sheet of copy paper I was turning into the roller.

I went out to the hall to get a drink of water from the cooler. Next to it was an open window facing east, and I looked out for a minute at the silver shimmers of heat-lightning playing over the lake. Even the sound of my office phone ringing didn't move me. Once in a while some pal will phone in a good tip that I can build a column around, but this just wasn't Diamond's night. Most likely the night operators were feeling the heat, too, and I'd get some character who'd want to talk to a Mr. Damon, or Dumond, or any other name that sounded something like mine but definitely was not.

But when I picked up the receiver, it was Artie Roth, my leg man and recent acquisition from the City News Bureau, my alma mater.

"I'm at the Chez," Artie said.

"And?"

"At a table right down front, Mr. Al Asperito and Mrs. Linda Dwight. Want it?"

I thought for a second. Al Asperito, not quite a criminal but almost caught several times. Among other things, he supposedly owned a lot of real estate over on West Madison. If you know the angles and play them right, there's plenty of profit to be made, even on Skid Row, and Mr. Al Asperito liked a lot more than four or five per cent on his money.

Mrs. Linda Dwight, young and not unbeautiful, was the wife of a wealthy distiller who had often been cited as an unseen force in state politics. Asperito and Linda Dwight definitely moved in different worlds, and I wondered what they were doing in a fancy night spot.

"Want it?" Artie repeated.

"I want it," I said. "Thanks." I sighed and pushed myself down at the typewriter, and forty-five minutes later I had a thousand little words, featuring the Asperito-Dwight thing, dressed up with the usual air of mystery and interrogation. I finished up with some stuff I'd gotten from a Hollywood producer at the Ambassador East that noon, jerked the paper out of the machine, reached for my cord jacket and hat. I left the column at the desk, took the elevator down nine floors and walked out on Michigan Avenue, into the hot cavernous night. I took the bus north to my apartment on Lakeside.

I showered, felt just as hot as ever, and poured some orange juice and gin over some ice cubes and tried to cool off with that. Finally I finished my drink and went to bed. I began to drowse, wondering if Al Asperito and Linda Dwight *did* add up to anything more than mildly sensational but insignificant gossip.

Naked on soggy sheets, I fell asleep. . . .

I felt more beat than ever in the morning. I got up around nine, walked over to Broadway, got my fifty-three Chevvy coupé out of the garage and drove down toward the paper. Yawning, I parked under Michigan Boulevard in a row of chrome and metal wagons more expensive than mine and walked up the long concrete stairway to the street level. The building towered high and tall against a colorless sky. Rosemary, my secretary, was already in the little office, and Artie was at the typewriter.

A couple of nice people to work with. Artie is twenty-one, skinny and black-haired with an engaging smile. His folks needed money, so he hadn't been able to afford college or journalism school. But he knew the territory, the big clubs and the hotels, and he kept good track of who came into town and who left it.

Rosemary McClennen is not a beautiful woman, but she is the kind of woman I'd marry if it weren't for some things. First, I had a sneaking idea that she was still in love with Joe McClennen, who exploded in a fighter plane over Korea. Second, I didn't feel like getting married anyway. It's a hell of a life for a woman, her husband being gone all hours of the night, the way I'd have to be. Rosemary has an eight-year-old son Tommy in the third grade, but she doesn't look it. Tall, slender, with long legs and tawny hair and clear skin and bright blue eyes, she takes to sheath skirts and frilly blouses that make her look her best. Rosemary and I had dinner now and then, sometimes at her apartment with Tommy there, and sometimes by ourselves at one of the half-dozen good spots downtown. The occasional dinners, however, hadn't once progressed to the border beyond which lay the country commonly labeled romance.

I pushed open the office door and a gust of hot air from a useless corner fan hit me. Artie looked up, grinned. Rosemary, standing at the window with a copy of the morning edition in her hands, turned and frowned a bit as she smiled.

"Ed Sullivan in person!" Artie said brightly.

"No, it isn't," I said.

"How do you expect me to get anywhere if you don't laugh at my stuff?"

"And where," I asked, "do you expect to get?"

Artie raised one hand, index finger pointed at the ceiling. "To the top," he said solemnly. "And don't come to me asking for a handout, because . . ." He stopped, as if slightly puzzled what to say next.

"In other words," I said, "you want a raise, and/ or a byline?" I scaled my hat onto a chair. "Not today, my friend. You're still a youngster."

"*Aagh!*" he growled at the typewriter.

I looked around the office. "That fan doesn't do much good," I said. Rosemary studied the morning edition, tapping the paper restlessly against her palm. "Hey," I said to her, "you don't seem very happy this morning. Artie and I knock ourselves out being fun—"

Artie waved deprecatingly at her. "She's just got the jumps. My father always says women worry too much."

I walked over to Rosemary and caught the fresh scent of her. Her blue eyes met mine for a moment, seriously, then flicked away. I saw that she had the paper open to my column. "What's the trouble, Rosemary?" I asked.

"Nothing," she said, with a quick intake of breath. Then she tried to force a smile onto her lips.

I shook my head gently. "Come on, now. I know that look." Her eyes shone with a concern I had seen there many times before; the ageless woman-worry for a man not taking care of himself. But this time the expression was more than worry over lack of galoshes or meals of hamburgers and malteds. That at once disturbed me, irritated me, and was gratifying; a three-fold emotion. But in this still, hot moment of the morning, the disturbance predominated.

"What is it?" I said softly.

"Well . . ." She drew her breath in quickly, as if she felt that the thing must come out for my own good. "This piece about Al Asperito bothers me, Harry."

"Why?" I said, sticking a cigarette in my mouth. "You mean it's too much off the beaten track of entertainment?"

She shook her head. Traffic sounded far below. "It's not that. It's—" She hesitated. "I suppose you'll call me a fool for even thinking such things, but I can't help it!"

"I won't. Go on."

"Well, you've used material before not quite in line with your usual. I don't know what it is, Harry. Something . . ." She uttered a helpless sigh. "Asperito's supposed to be a criminal, and out with another man's wife, too. Asperito might be the kind of man to take offense."

I was startled. "You mean he might make a complaint?"

"Not just a complaint." Her cheeks reddened as if she felt instinctively that she was right but was being shamed into a feeling of foolishness.

I patted her shoulder. "Rosemary, even if Asperito is a criminal, he won't use the tactics of the twenties just because I put him in the column. Nothing's going to happen."

"Damn you!" she said intensely, crumpling the paper. She turned her back, defiantly and stood staring

blindly out the window. I felt uneasy, and a little embarrassed. She had been trying to help, but instinctively I rebelled against such mothering tactics and
dismissed her fears as silly and meaningless.

"Besides, it was so hot last night, and . . ." I began
loudly, but realized that it was a poor excuse. I
picked my apartment key out of my pocket and
started whirling the chain as I stared at the wall.
Halfway between belt and apartment key hung my
only public display of fame, a Sigma Delta Chi key
from college. She was right on one point, of course.
I usually left the criminal element alone. Judgment,
I thought, the heat sure gives you a kick in the pants
and you're mightily confused. Well, there was nothing much I could do at the moment. If there were re-
percussions, I would hear from higher up.

But the atmosphere between us remained tense
and charged. Tentatively I reached out and touched
Rosemary's shoulder. She faced me, reshaping a smile
onto her lips. "Look," I said haltingly, "I'm sorry if
I don't seem to pay much attention. I apologize. I—
I appreciate your wanting to help," I finished
weakly.

Her eyes met mine. "I wish you did," she said earnestly. Then her smile deepened and the tension relaxed. "You've got work to do," she said. "The city
awaits those pearls of wisdom. . . ."

My desk pad told me I was to lunch at the Berghoff
with a local industrialist interested in getting a little
home-grown theater started in Chicago. I retrieved
my hat and started for the door.

"Hey, genius," Rosemary said. I turned. "Do us a

favor and take care of yourself, will you?" Then she laughed as if she had said something silly.

There was heavy truck traffic in the roadway under Michigan when I got there. I opened my car door, started to get in and stopped. Someone had taken a thick black wax crayon and lettered on the inside of the windshield:

Lay off, Diamond.

A huge semi- went thundering by over the bricks, echoes bouncing back between the concrete pillars. Something whizzed by my head in the same instant that I heard a faint popping sound. I ducked and looked down the rows of parked automobiles. Then my gaze swung up to the windshield. A starred pattern had appeared there, to the left of the message, and a large chip of glass had been sliced away. I dug around on the floor of the car and found a small slug, the kind used in a target pistol I had owned when I was in high school. I weighed it in my hand, slid back out of the car and dropped the slug onto the bricks, staring at it for a moment. I examined the surrounding area again and saw no one. I felt that the shot had not been intended to hit me, only to add emphasis to the message.

Asperito? Who else could it be? But, lay off what? I couldn't quite reconcile such extreme measures with a frankly gossipy item in a newspaper column. But I had a mild case of stomach queasiness for a moment. I had stepped over the line and gotten warned. Then I felt a burn of anger. I didn't have any affection for unseen pistol artists, no matter how small a caliber the weapon. I started chipping the wax crayon away with my fingernail, looking around some more. Probably he'd slipped in and out of the car as if he owned it, and no one had noticed. Then a patient wait as he hid behind one of the pillars until I came along, and with the truck roar filling the road, the shot would pass relatively unheard. I didn't like it.

I got all the crayon off and started the motor.

Chapter II

My luncheon companion was hot on restoring the theater to the town, but I couldn't care less. Even the Berghoff's usually delicious *Sauerbraten* went gritty and tasteless on my tongue, and I had trouble downing my beer. At last the man looked at his watch and decided it was time to go. He pumped my hand and said he hoped I'd give his idea a good play and I said, Sure I would. I sat there alone for a while, vaguely aware of the bright, brittle chatter of the luncheon crowd around me. I felt not bright but brittle.

Things at the time were peculiar. O'Riordan, the State Attorney, was near to death with a malignancy, and had been for some four months. Up until then he had been working, or so I understood from my friends at the paper, on a major sweep of the town's rackets. One of his assistants, Victor Quinn by name, had been sitting in the big man's chair the past four months, unable to fill it physically or any other way. There had been an increase of crime during that period, and from bits I'd heard, all the vultures were roosting on the tree limb, waiting for O'Riordan to die. My main source of information, Charlie Parnell, a veteran police reporter of twenty-odd years' service, said that while crime was on the upswing, things definitely were not organized. Charlie was of the opinion that if things ever did get organized, the whole town would bleed money out of its pores. Where did all this wraith-like theory get me? Not a solitary place. Al Asperito was a hood, but I had no interest in the organization of the city's crime machine. I only had an interest in my own skin.

Deciding I was getting nowhere, I paid my check, walking out onto Adams into a drizzle like lukewarm water from a garden sprinkling can. I drove north to Wrigley Field. Though the Cubs lost through a couple of fumble-footed errors, the action took my mind off the writing on my windshield, and the shot.

I grabbed a 'burger across the boulevard from the paper, then went up to my office. It was a little after six; both Artie and Rosemary were gone. I threw up the window and let the rain blow in, cooling things faintly, while I wrote a thousand uninspired words about night-life in and north of the Loop, using that time-worn device of "today and yesterday." Not that a little local history isn't all right occasionally, but something almost like a wad of smoldering rags sogged the life out of my brain, yet made me tense as a wire at the same time.

I turned in my copy and drove out to catch the eight-thirty show in the Edgewater Beach's Marine Room. My near-unintelligible notes taken, I drove south again, a copy of a rival paper on the seat beside me, folded to the entertainment page. It advertised a semi-famous female vocalist at one of the near north-side clubs, opening tonight. I stared through the rain at nothing and decided to give it a try.

The Riff Club was sandwiched between two old

apartments near Chicago Avenue. For a heavy price you could soak up the atmosphere, which included artists and poets, both pre-success and post-failure, and an occasional name of the stage or Hollywood.

The female vocalist was Beginning the Beguine in an amber spot, and twisting the melody all out of line. Liking straight melody lines, I jotted down things and hunched over my beer until the lights came up. Then I swiveled on my stool and looked out over the table area, about half full, as the applause rippled and died. Three Gary, Indiana, Latins began rattling gourds and tapping drums for the rhumba enthusiasts. At first I saw no one in the crowd I recognized. But a closer look corrected that impression.

Linda Dwight had already seen me, and her black eyes fastened on me over the half-dozen tables between us. She was sitting, twirling a glass in coral-tipped fingers, her head cocked slightly to one side. Black poodled hair, a rather flat face, but an attractive mouth, a slender neck, and that concave sweep of breasts down to a point, then a lush underslung ripening folded in by the gold lamé dress. There was a man with her, a few years past her thirty, and I knew her husband, William Dwight, was at least twenty years older.

She kept her eyes on me momentarily, and they were mocking me, challenging me, asking, do you dare me? My drink had produced a pleasantly warm glow in my stomach and a lazy languor as if I was some kind of oiled fighting machine, ready, competent, but relaxed until action was called for. I looked hard at her as I set my glass on the bar, and she knew I dared her. Her mouth moved as she spoke to her partner, but her eyes never flickered from mine.

I stood up and smoothed out my suit as best I could while Al Asperito got up from the table. He was coming toward me, maroon studs on his white shirt winking like three eyes. His sallow face seemed pinched and determined, and he rolled his thin shoulders slightly. Linda Dwight was now avidly studying her glass. The rhumba drums rattled like dice thrown on wood, and Al Asperito stopped a pace in front of me.

I pulled my hand from my coat pocket and held out an opened pack of cigarettes to Asperito. His hands stayed at his side as I lit one for myself. "You want to see me," I said. "And I don't have to guess about what."

Asperito's tense, thin face seemed to tremble with strain. He slid onto a bar stool and licked his lips. "Diamond," he said in a scratchy voice, "I didn't like what you wrote about me and Mrs. Dwight in your article yesterday morning."

"I guessed that much."

Asperito drew his breath in suddenly, then shook his head, as if he had trouble controlling himself. "Diamond, you don't seem to get my drift. Now I'm not objecting to being mentioned as Mrs. Dwight's escort, it's just that you imply too damned much. You got a way of hinting, of twisting those words, Diamond, like you're peeking through a keyhole, or something."

"Ruins your character," I said flatly. I glanced over at the Dwight woman, studying her glass as if it were a nuclear physics problem. "But I don't think you've got all that character you're worried about. Nobody does. You're news. That ought to flatter you."

"It don't," Asperito said sourly.

"I've got a better idea for a column than the one last night," I said slowly. "Al Asperito, prominent plunger in Skid Row properties and West Madison Street estates, writes notes on reporters' windshields, and takes pot shots from behind pillars."

"What the hell are you talking about?" he grumbled.

"The message you put on my car, like some hood out of the twenties!" I said. "Telling me to lay off. Why don't you cut out looking at those old gangster movies on TV? Read a good book instead."

"I wrote nothing on your car, Diamond."

"I say you did. I say you also shot at me this morning."

"That calls me a liar, Diamond."

"Take it that way if you want to."

I wasn't quite ready for him, but I got ready, fast. With a sudden snort of breath, he swiftly dropped into a crouch and his right fist blurred at my belly. I used my left to deflect the blow and gave him the same treatment with my right. He shook his head and tottered. The bartender made a loud complaint and I grabbed Asperito's neck and shoved him hard against the bar. He let out all his breath at once. I ignored the bartender and turned and walked away, after catching a glimpse of Linda Dwight. Her expression had changed to one of amusement. The maître d' gave me a cold stare as I stalked through the foyer, massaging my knuckles and feeling partially satisfied. I figured my free admission, or any admission for me, to the Riff Club was at an end.

My watch showed only ten o'clock, but I felt as if it were twelve hours later. I drove slowly up the Outer Drive, playing jigsaw puzzle with my thoughts. Angles didn't fit. Asperito was not a good actor. He couldn't act the polished gentleman any more than he could act the smooth liar. He seemed genuinely angered by my accusation.

The thing that bothered me was that if Asperito hadn't written the warning, someone else had. And for a different reason. Someone did not want Al Asperito and Linda Dwight connected in print. Would it be William Dwight? The why escaped me, but I felt that if I knew why, I'd know something I should be smart enough to forget. But then, I'd never been very smart.

I went to bed that night with no answers. I didn't even have any questions—good ones, that is. I didn't dream, but I awoke several times, and even though the air was superheated and saturated with moisture, my skin felt chilly. Rain dripped down from the top of the window, the street light catching it, an alchemy of darkness and street lamps making each drop a tear of gold, round and shimmering. The gold droplets broke on the sill with a faint sound, and I likened the fall and the breaking to a certain newspaperman named Diamond if he should get too nosey. But then I reminded myself that first, I actually knew very little; and second, my apprehensions were vague and indefinite, or nearly so.

But apprehensions they remained. I couldn't shake

them all through the hot night when my skin crawled with chill.

In the morning I learned what the world had been doing while I lay in darkness. I walked into the lobby of the building about ten to see Charlie Parnell buying a pack of cigarettes at the counter under the big clock. I walked over and hit him on the shoulder. He turned around. I saw that I shouldn't have been so friendly.

Charlie Parnell was tall and spare, a bachelor, a paradoxical person. He read nothing for pleasure except philosophy, and his own stories after he wrote them. Plato mattered to him, and Christ and Spinoza and Kant and Whitehead. You could see Charlie Parnell's twenty years on the police beat; you could see it in the tired stoop of his shoulders under the neat but worn blue suit, in the tired brown eyes behind steel-rimmed glasses. Charlie had been offered better jobs on the paper, but something drew him to police stations, the same way something drew him to philosophy. He was interested, I think, in the struggle between good and evil. And he knew where to find them both, firsthand.

Charlie frowned at me, his eyes seeming imprisoned behind the glass walls of his lenses. "Hey," I said softly, "what happened? Your philosophical system go to hell?"

Charlie stared at me. "You hear?"

"About what?" I said as we walked into the elevator. The door slid closed and the elevator boy gave Charlie a frown. He'd heard, too.

"O'Riordan," Charlie said. "Died in the hospital last night." His voice took on new earnestness though his tone grew no louder. "Harry, do you know that this is what every one of them has been waiting for? And the assistant D.A.'s no better. He'll leave O'Riordan's files untouched, the yellow little . . ." The elevator stopped and the door slid open. "My floor," he said to the air. "See you." The door closing cut him from view, a sad spare man who hunted the jungle of his own mind for answers.

I reflected that what he said was probably true. Charlie was in a position to know what went on in the city. Wondering just what bearing O'Riordan's death had on me, I got off the elevator. Rosemary looked more concerned than ever when I entered the office. Artie wasn't in yet. I scaled my hat onto a chair and waited for her to speak.

"It's all over the building, Harry," she said.

I sat down at the desk and looked at my blank pad. "You mean O'Riordan?"

"Oh." Her throat made a small catching sound. "No, I didn't mean that, although people have been talking. You and Al Asperito, last night."

I got up and took her shoulders between my hands. "Look," I said. "I ran into him last night by chance. He threw the first punch."

"I know, Harry. It's just the idea—"

"The idea," I interrupted, "is that you should stop making like you're worried or something." I grinned at her. She didn't grin back.

"Or something," she said, turning and pulling gently out from under my grip. That woman! I thought exasperatedly. I could almost fall in love with her, but then she mothers me too damned much, and I need a mother like a hole in the head. And I thought of Al Asperito and knew I needed no holes that he might supply at all. I didn't exactly change the subject but I started off on a different tack.

"The man upstairs complain about me?" I asked. "Employees brawling, et cetera?"

A quick tight shake of her head. "No, Harry. The way I heard the story, from Carney, the new rewrite man, you had already been accounted for as having defended yourself."

"I'm glad my purity remains unblemished," I said, not feeling as chipper as I sounded.

I spent the rest of the day in the cubbyhole office, working ahead on a couple of columns. Rosemary didn't broach the subject of the Asperito affair again, but she moved and talked as if she were under a threatening rain cloud without an umbrella.

The sky filled with the actual clouds I had imagined hovering over Rosemary, and toward four, swollen and black, they broke and poured down real rain in fierce slanting columns. I left the office about six, drove on into the Loop, dawdled over a steak until eight, then caught a recently opened comedy at the Erlanger. There in the cavern beyond the lights, the witty stage patter wasn't particularly funny, and all the actors had a way of looking like Al Asperito. For the second night running I slept badly.

Next morning, I found an answer to the mixture of fatigue, boredom and vague fear united inside my office. Artie, busy at the typewriter, gave me a nod as I walked in, and I glanced over at the heavy man heaving himself up from the chair. He wore a cheap bright blue suit, badly pressed, a pink necktie and a shirt with a sweated gray neckband. Fingers like cigars held a wilted Panama, and his look had a touch of whimsy in it, because an expression of Polite Interest, which he must have thought belonged to meetings of this sort, seemed sleepy and childlike on his ham of a face with its thick purple nose.

He stuck out the right hand. "Tripp, Mr. Diamond; Pat Tripp." I shook hands with him, feeling the sweat, and he frowned as if he didn't know the next step. "This is confidential," he said, glancing at Artie. Artie got up and walked out of the office. I shut the door after him.

"Now, Mr. Tripp," I said, in the chair behind the desk, cigarette going. Mr. Pat Tripp bothered me, because the cut of the suit, the too-large stone on his right little finger that glowed like a diamond but wasn't, marked him as someone out of a special world I didn't want to meddle with.

Tripp sat down again. "I work for Mr. Asperito," he said. I stared pointedly at Tripp, waiting. "Al wanted me to arrange a meeting, Mr. Diamond. He didn't want to come in here himself; didn't want to phone. So he sent me."

"What sort of meeting?"

"Al has some information that he thinks your paper might be interested in. That's all he told me to say. He says if you're interested, you should come to his home tonight. At nine-thirty."

I stared at my cigarette, its smoke snaking up like a hangrope into humid air. I told myself, Nuts! half rationally, but I felt a grim excitement, too, because I couldn't help believing that this might tie in with the crayon message, the shot and the reason someone besides Asperito wanted no connections between him and the Dwight fortune. Then, too, I figured it could be a sucker trap, baited out of a revenge motive; but curiosity has killed a lot more humans than cats.

"Give me the address and tell your boss that I'll be there at nine-thirty."

Tripp smiled proudly, childishly delighted at his own accomplishment of an important mission, took a thumb-marked card out of his pocket and wrote out an address on North Sacramento near Devon. He handed it over, allowed me to shake his hand and left. As soon as the door closed behind him, I called Charlie Parnell's desk.

"Diamond, Charlie. Know a Pat Tripp? Connected with Al Asperito?"

"Fatsy Patsy Tripp. Big, purple nose. Childish."

"That fits him," I said. "Thanks."

"Stick to theaters and night-club reviews," Charlie said sourly. "They're safer."

I told him I would and hung up. Barring a trap, apparently Al Asperito wanted to give out information. Then either his anger at me had cooled unnaturally soon, or else he had generated new anger. Hell, I didn't know. But I had a rather strong desire to meet the guy who had triggered the target pistol. I listened to the fan until Artie came back, one inch deeper into something than I had been when he'd left me with Tripp.

Chapter III

The hours dragged on like lead weights rolling down an incline toward a goal that was the next hour. I sweated the minutes, one by one, and then the hands of my watch showed the new hour and another touchdown had been made. I was glad that Rosemary's job gave her a day off in the middle of the week, because I didn't want her to know I was going to call on Asperito.

I got through the day and returned to my apartment. I fried some hamburgers, drank a beer and put Cole Porter on the player, but I couldn't rid myself of an itch to walk from wall to wall, or to chainsmoke cigarettes, or to look at my watch, hoping it would be an hour later, when I knew I had looked at it less than a minute before. The sky over the Drive turned a deep gray, then a soggy black. I stood in the darkness now, not having turned on the lights, and felt my shirt plaster itself clammily to my belly. I raised my watch, and the green numerals glowed at nine-five. Figuring twenty minutes to drive to Asperito's, I would still be early, but why should Asperito mind? I put on a fresh open-throated sport shirt, grabbed my coat and went out.

I drove five miles over the legal speed limit

through the steaming black night, up Sheridan to Devon and west to Sacramento, where I turned left into a sparsely settled district. Only one or two bungalows stood on each block, the rest of the blocks being taken up with black fields of weeds and a few unhealthy trees. I checked the address again on the card Tripp had given me. On my right in the block ahead stood a low brick bungalow. I made a quick mental estimate and decided that it was the place. I pulled into the curb and lit a cigarette. Street lights ranged a block apart, and since the house was in the center of its block and set far back, thick black shadows cloaked it. In the next block I could make out the shape of another automobile parked on my side. Nine twenty-six, the green watch numerals said. I noticed a light in the front room of the bungalow, shining behind tightly shuttered Venetian blinds.

The sound came like a champagne cork popping and my fingers tightened on the wheel. I got out, circled the car and started for the bungalow at a run. Halfway up the front yard I stopped, listening. Weeds crackled to my left, back along the side of the house. I started forward again, edging toward the house corner and walking with small steps toward the rear, tight in to the wall. My own feet rattled in a patch of weeds and I stopped, my heart beginning to slug faster. Three feet down the wall, a raised window threw a three-inch patch of yellow across the ground. I thought I could make out something bulking away from the wall beyond it, but the contrast of the light in all that black made my sight play tricks on me. Cautiously I took one pace forward. The shadows stirred beyond the window. I ducked low to the left away from the wall and ran forward. The shadows broke and black shoes flashed in the light and the other man came for me, out in the weeds where no light fell. Looking up from a low crouch, I could see him against the dimly lighted sky, almost shapeless, seeming of monstrous size from the distorted angle. I dived forward to tackle him and a toe caught me viciously alongside the jaw, and spun me over backward into the weeds. The man leaped for me and I rolled. A foot thudded down where my head had been.

I grabbed for the leg and it began to wriggle fiercely, as if I were a dog chewing at the mailman's trousers. I hung on, my jaw aching, my head ringing. The leg shook free, and I got one knee under me and started to scramble up. The air parted with a swift sigh and a heavy gun barrel cracked across my temple. Pinwheels exploded behind my eyes. My face was pressed in the weeds, and I heard someone take off in a rapid run. I felt myself going into darkness, and I tried shaking my head. The running sounds vanished in the direction where I dimly heard a motor cough to life, and I figured that the shadow-man had gotten in the car down in the next block. A burr prickled my left cheek. I raised myself on my elbows and fell back down again, blacking out.

When consciousness filtered back, I got on my feet, checked my watch. Not more than fifteen minutes had passed since I arrived. I turned and walked toward the bar of light from under the Venetian blind. I crouched down and looked in on Al Asperito's bedroom, furnished with twin Hollywoods, a dresser and a desk.

One shaded lamp had fallen off a night table between the beds, and it lay throwing its light in the corner. I saw no sign of Asperito, but after a moment I caught the sound of heavy breathing. I ran around to the front and the door opened under my hand. I went through the softly lighted living room, the dinette, along a hall, then I was looking into the bedroom, and down at Al Asperito, where he lay on the floor between the two beds. He was drawn up fetuslike, his arms wrapped around his stomach. He'd opened the bedroom window for ventilation, and he'd gotten it, all right; with a silenced gun.

I stepped inside, jerked down the Venetian blind. When I turned back I saw the dark blood seeping out from under Asperito. He was breathing. I knelt by him, turned his head. He groaned, recognized me.

"Up . . ." he gasped. I lifted him as gently as I could, and he swayed heavily, still with his arms wrapped around his stomach, unable to unwind himself from his hunched agony. I managed to get him into a chair. Beneath his forearms blood smeared his shirt just above his belt.

I got a cigarette going and stuck it between his lips. His eyes caught mine, telling me that he knew he was dying. He coughed and groaned so I took away the cigarette, and his indrawn breath sounded like spent surf hissing on the sand.

"Diamond," he whispered, "I didn't see anybody. Silencer." He closed his eyes for a few seconds, then opened them. "We got to talk, Diamond," he whispered.

"Sure," I said. "But I'll call an ambulance first. We'll talk at the hospital."

"Talk now," he insisted. "Phone's—in the hall."

I conned the nearest hospital into sending an ambulance, then got Central Homicide, Captain Mario Tocca's office. I gave the sergeant there Asperito's address and told him to relay it to Captain Tocca at once. When I got back to the bedroom, I thought that Asperito was dead. Panic ran through me until I saw the slow labored rise and fall of his chest. I shook his jaw gently and his eyes blinked open. "The ambulance is on the way," I said.

Asperito ran his tongue across his lips, gulped more air. I eased myself down on one of the beds, waiting. "Got to talk," he repeated. "You—you write this down."

I got out my pad and pencil. Asperito winced. "Be all right—minute," he wheezed. "Don't feel so good."

I waited.

Finally his eyes focused on me, and he pulled a deep breath. "Diamond," he began, "maybe you think I'm nuts, wanting to talk to you. I'll try to explain my idea."

Each word came at the price of painful labor, one syllable dropping on another as if he had to force his throat to sound them. "Last night," he croaked, "some people had a meeting. Important meeting. I was there."

"Where?"

"William Dwight's place. Wilmette." That was something to write down. "Six of us. Sitting around the big table in Dwight's den. . . ." His eyes wandered over the wall, then came back to mine.

"Who was there, Al?"

"Milo Heinz—runs the bookies and policy in town. And Bill Dwight. Respectable now. Big bootlegger, back in twenties. Likes to invest, if you know what I mean. Then there was Big Roy Roblein. High-priced dames. Jake Bushnell, dope. And me— you know, slum tenements." He lay back gasping for a moment, then gathered himself again. "You got that down? Good. Oh, yeah. Then there was Otto Schloss —sort of a wholesaler in hoods. Hired guns, strike-breakers, muscle guys, you name it. . . ." Asperito groaned and lay back, panting for breath, his fingers curved convulsively at his belt buckle.

After a few minutes he began again, but he was getting weaker. "Dwight got us all together. I don't like to go out on rainy nights, but I went because I had a good idea what Dwight wanted. With O'Riordan dead and that jerk Quinn trying to handle things, Dwight figured it was a good time to organize. Wanted to finance a regular company or something, with us as directors. Make things run more efficient.

"Up to now, all the little pitches were separate, each guy grabbing top hand and holding. Scared outa their pants, Diamond, by O'Riordan. He had us all on the run. . . . Now what Dwight wanted to do wasn't a bad idea, Diamond. All the others thought it was okay, too. All of a sudden, the funniest thing. The lights went out."

I frowned. "Rainy night," I said. "Could be a power failure."

"No—no. It wasn't funny. They went out all over the house, and everybody was swearing and hollering, then they went on again. It was so quiet all you could hear was the rain outside. And then someone swore and pointed to the middle of the table, to this piece of paper. We could all read what was typed on it, because we were all on one side of the table. Nobody said a word. We read it, and Diamond, I got scared. I can't remember the exact words. . . ." Asperito's eyes wandered again, as if the words might appear like the handwriting on the wall. "Yeah, it was sorta like this: 'I am in this room and I am working for the Eastern syndicate. We're moving in and we'll do our own organizing and our own collecting.' " Asperito's eyes were ghostly hollows of memory. "Then it said that we'd better string along or we'd all get hurt. Nobody had signed it. We sat there looking at each other, and I guess everybody was trying to figure who'd slipped it on the table when the lights went out. The paper'd been folded, you could see that. I looked at all the guys and I couldn't pick the one, and I *still* can't, Diamond. I don't know who in hell put that note there. . . ."

I was writing fast on my pad. Now, at last, I was beginning to get an idea of why I'd been warned off with the crayon message and the shot. This thing was big enough to swallow cities at one gulp. And I was sitting right in the big ugly middle of it.

"What happened after that?" I asked.

Asperito licked his lips. He was having a tougher time trying to talk every moment, with his life draining away under his hands. Then his voice came again, weaker than before.

"We talked about it. About how it must be some practical joke, but I didn't think so and nobody else did, either; not really. So then Dwight asked what did we think about the syndicate doing the organizing. Believe me, we may get pretty mean around here, but we don't get mean the way they do. Anyhow, I got sore. I said that I didn't want guys I'd never seen muscle their way into town and tell me what to do and how to run my business and collect twenty per cent of my take, just because I was too chicken to do anything about it.

"Then that Jake Bushnell opened up. I always had him tagged as yellow, and he said, Sure, we ought to throw in because he didn't want to wind up dead, and he knew how the syndicate worked. So I told him that we should tell the syndicate to go to hell."

He glanced down at his wet red fingers clamped across his middle. "I guess the guy that did this heard me say it. But I said I was sore and I was. The way Dwight had it planned, we'd all get more than we were making right now. But the other way, with the syndicate moving in—well, none of us would be making near what we did before, on our own."

He asked for another cigarette, and when I gave it to him, he shook with a ragged fit of coughing. For a minute I stood taut, thinking that this time it was curtains for sure. But the coughing rattled away and he motioned to me to sit down again.

"Well," I asked, "what did you decide?"

He shook his head. "Nothing. The others wanted to think about it. Dwight said there wasn't much point in talking about it any more right then, so we all went home. And that's it, Diamond."

I frowned at my scrawled pages of notes. "I don't quite see why you wanted me to have this, Al. What can I do?"

"You could put it in the paper, Diamond. I guess—I guess now that I think of it, it wasn't so smart. But I figured maybe we could make a deal. You can print only so much in your column, or any place in the whole paper, I don't care. You know, don't use any names like mine or Dwight or Otto Schloss. But just tell enough so that the syndicate might get scared off." Asperito's face looked like a sweaty, glistening skull in the crooked light from the fallen lamp. "I wanted to keep the business private, sort of among friends, right here in town. I guess it was a pretty poor try, though." He glanced down at his scarlet hands and shook his head. "Damn, Diamond, I never knew a slug could hurt so much." He closed his eyes, speaking as if in a trance. "I always was a loudmouth, Diamond. Whoever—" He gasped for air. "Whoever put that note on the table last night figured he'd make me an example, I guess. For the rest of them."

That sounded sensible, but I also remembered Tripp in my office, and I suspected that the man who put the note on the table had also wanted to keep any mention of all this out of the papers. I had a conviction that the killing had a double-barreled motive. An example, yes, but it was a means of shutting Asperito's mouth, too. Fatsy Patsy Tripp had talked; I'd stake money on it. And he had talked after he'd been in my office.

I was about to remind Asperito of Tripp's visit, when I heard a siren sounding from the south, getting closer. I stuffed my notes in my shirt pocket just as the siren growled to silence before the house. Asperito's eyelids flickered, and I started for the front door. It was the ambulance, and I pointed the way back to the kid in the white coat.

I'd just started a cigarette when the kid came back to the doorway. "He's dead," he said flatly.

Chapter IV

He hesitated, apparently waiting for orders. I told him that the police were due to arrive any time, and he decided to go back out to the ambulance for a smoke.

Another car slid to a halt in front. I held the door open for Captain Mario Tocca. He stepped inside, a man of average build, olive skin, jutting black eyebrows and thick black hair. His tan suit and white shirt showed the ravages of humidity and sweat. He hoisted a wet cigar to his narrow lips and a gold wedding band glinted for a moment. Then he stepped past me into the living room. I could see the flare of a cigarette in the black police Ford parked at the curb. I shut the door while Tocca glanced about the room. "What have you got, Diamond?" he asked. "You didn't make it clear on the phone."

"Al Asperito, Captain. He's been murdered."

Tocca's eyebrows lifted in surprise. I gestured toward the bedroom, and followed his quick stride to the doorway. Asperito's head had slumped forward onto his chest, but other than that his position remained unchanged. Tocca advanced, knelt down and touched a finger to the man's cheek. He bent over to peer at the wound under the bloody buddha hands.

37

Then he straightened, and went to the phone and called headquarters, requesting the medical examiner and the usual team of print and photograph men.

He asked me to come into the front room. "Sit down, Diamond, will you?" he said. "Did you call the ambulance?"

"Yes. I couldn't tell how badly Asperito had been hit. I thought he might have a chance."

"Sure, okay," Tocca said. He went out to the ambulance and in a moment I heard the motor start up and the sound of it heading south on Sacramento. Tocca returned, took another glance around the room and settled himself into the green plastic chair. He was carrying a notebook.

"Diamond," he said tactfully, "your newspaper has always found the police department very co-operative, and that's the way it should be." A faint suggestion of tired mockery appeared in his eyes. "I'm well aware of the power you've got to back you up." He didn't need to add that everyone from the Commissioner down would start to dance if the presses began rolling the wrong way. "I appreciate your calling us right away," he concluded.

"Asperito did some talking," I said. "That's why he had me out here." I held my notes up in the air. "I've got it down."

"Do I get it?" Tocca asked quietly.

I debated it mentally, but saw no reason for not giving him something. "Sure," I said.

"Let's have it, then," Tocca said, methodically unscrewing his fountain pen and preparing to write.

I got to my feet and walked to the front door. "It

doesn't start with what I've got written down. It goes back a couple of days."

Tocca nodded, his pen poised. "Anywhere you want to start it, Diamond."

I told him the whole story, from Artie's first phone call, through the one-blow brawl with Asperito, the fight outside the house and the things Asperito had told me. There was a ten-minute interruption when the headquarters people arrived and Tocca conferred with them in the bedroom. At the end of the story, though, Tocca showed signs of being shaken. "Well!" he said. He stood up. "Can I have your notes, Diamond? I'll return them. I'd just like to check to see that I got everything clear."

I passed him the pad. Suddenly he exploded with bulldog ferocity, "Good God, Diamond! This is a package of pure dynamite. With O'Riordan dead and Quinn holding down his chair, anything's liable to happen. I'll tell you off the record that Quinn's got us all spitting blue down at headquarters for fear the town'll open up wide. He's just too small for the job."

He hadn't broached the subject of newspaper release, so I kept silent on it, too. I said, "I'm not too much of an expert on such things, Captain, but I imagine the syndicate wouldn't make things any easier."

"You're right, they wouldn't!" Tocca said. He threw his dead cigar into an ash stand, approached me, one finger bobbing emphatically before him. "Compared with conditions in the twenties here in Chicago, we've been fairly well off for the past few years. Dwight's system would make it worse. But with the syndicate in control, it would be terrible. The syndicate *plus* Quinn would make this town a breeding ground for every hood trying to make a dirty dollar!"

"What burns me," I said, "is that I had the killer right in my hands and I let him get away."

"Hell," Tocca said, "how were you supposed to know?" The wire-basket boys came through from the bedroom carrying Asperito's sheeted body. Tocca watched them go out, then shook his head sadly. "I hate to see anybody bumped. A human body's a wonderful thing."

"Captain," I said slowly, "about the story for the paper . . . ?"

His fists tightened and the film of sweat on his forehead seemed to grow heavier in a space of seconds. "You know you've got me over a barrel, don't you?"

I nodded. "That's right. I imagine you don't want this Dwight business played up. Or even mentioned. I doubt if you want more than a story on Asperito's death: 'The unknown assailant . . . the police have several important leads . . .' that sort of stuff?"

"You're pretty smart," Tocca said in a flat voice.

"I'm willing to make a deal," I said carefully.

Tocca smiled wryly. "Deals-schmeals! You think I owe you something, Diamond? Well, so I do. But I wish to God I didn't!" He was only half sore; otherwise he might have managed a full smile. But the heat and the import of Asperito's death had weighted his mind.

"Want to hear what I've got to offer, Captain?"

"Go ahead," he said, sucking noisily on his cigar and relighting it.

"I want to sit in on the investigation," I said slowly. "I've got a stake in this thing now, Captain. I'd be willing to bet that the man who put the note on the table at Dwight's was the same man who wrote on my windshield and fired the shot at me. I don't like being shot at. I don't like being slugged and kicked. He's one man, I'm one man; that makes it even. I want him."

"In return for?" Tocca asked with ill-concealed cynicism.

"For a simple story that Asperito was found dead, foul play suspected, et cetera. And I get the exclusive on the final story when it's wrapped up. Twelve hours or twenty-four, depending on which way it works out best for the paper."

Tocca's face darkened as he bit down hard on the fraying cigar. "What am I supposed to do? Complain? I wish I could make you newspaper guys learn what police business is; that once in a great while it's a little more important than peddling the public prints. You and your lousy stories!"

I did a slow boil. "Right now," I ground out, "I'm not after a story. I'm merely trying to tell you that I *am* after a man who tries to scare me with a threatening message, who tries to shoot me, and then tonight, right outside this house, slugs me and then gives me a working over with his boots."

Someone—and I wish I knew who—had dealt me into this at the very start, and whatever happened from now on, I didn't intend to quit. I'd run down every little lead I could get, remember every minor detail I could cram in my head, in order to pull up the man hanging on the end of that thread of murder. My feeling concerned the city, too, but only in a minor way. They, the city's people, deserved something a little better than a club over the head from nowhere if the syndicate clamped down.

But a newspaperman takes a certain obscure pride in his job. The man had picked his victim in the wrong profession. I was willing to let Captain Mario Tocca shut up both me and my newspaper for a chance to get that unknown killer who figured he could shut us up in other ways.

"Now," Tocca said sourly, "if you're all puffed up with the Dick Tracy juice, you can come along and stick your nose in. I'm going to start with Dwight." He kept talking as we went out of the house and down to the squad car. I climbed in the back seat, Tocca gave instructions to the heavy-set sergeant, and we started north on Sacramento toward William Dwight's home in Wilmette.

"The only way I can see to do this thing is to find Asperito's killer and then dump the evidence into Quinn's lap," Tocca said to me over his shoulder. I sensed that he was straightening out his own thoughts, rather than providing me with his method of operation. "If we can find out who's playing the part of the seventh man, the syndicate contact, and pin the killing on him, then we've got a weapon to stop the syndicate."

The phrase "the seventh man" stuck in my mind as a good one to use in my copy, if I ever got around to writing the story. "Of course," I said, "we can't be sure that this seventh man was actually the one that shot Asperito."

"No, *I* can't be sure," Tocca admitted. I let the slur pass. "But I'm wondering if the syndicate might think that was the best way to work it. If this one man fails to establish the groundwork successfully he can be killed, the loss to the syndicate is small, and the chances of any information leaks are lessened. I think you had him, Diamond. One of those five men at Dwight's last night—barring theatrical junk like a hole in the ceiling to lower a note through—put the note on the table, heard Asperito's beef, and decided to kill him. Four of the men at the meeting had to think it over, and from there it's a downhill road to giving in."

He lapsed into silence. The car rolled east on Devon, turned into Sheridan where Broadway ended and slid north past the bulk of the Granada Theatre, the El, and the rows of lakeside apartments. The seventh man would be the one who put the crayon message on my windshield and fired at me, wanting no hint at all of any city-wide organization to leak out.

The squad car swung past the shadowed campus of Northwestern and on up beyond the big lighted homes that crouched far back on wide lawns. When we passed the white sign announcing Wilmette, Tocca had the car slowed and we went to work looking for the numerals that would spell out Dwight's home. "Here it is," Tocca said abruptly. The driver swung to the right, slowing the car up a concrete drive and under a portico beside the house and a long black lawn. Tocca and I got out of the car and walked around the red brick house to the front porch. Tocca punched a button and two chimes sounded in some muted distance.

A small gray-haired woman in a black rustling dress opened the door. Her rabbit face was defensive. "Yes?"

"Police," Tocca said, flipping his wallet open and shut. "Is Mr. Dwight home?"

"Yes, sir. Please come in." We went into a small reception hall furnished with a table and one tall-backed ancient chair, its blackened wood glowing with a high sheen like the chair of a king. Well, Dwight and the others were kings of a sort, in their own circle. "Mr. Dwight is in the den," the woman said tonelessly. "Please follow me."

She knocked softly at a brace of tall doors leading right from the hall. A deep, vibrant voice rumbled admittance. She opened the door, blocking our way. "Two gentlemen from the police, Mr. Dwight."

Dwight's deep voice said, "Let them in, Helen." The woman stepped aside, and Tocca preceded me into the den, the room in which, last night, the seventh man had showed his hand.

Long and windowless, with a desk at one end and a television console at the other, the room's walls consisted of bookcases from floor to ceiling, filled with current volumes whose worn jackets showed someone in the ex-bootlegger's home liked to read. Midway down the left wall was a long polished oak table, and six matching armchairs stood between the table and the bookcase, as if the meeting had just broken up. One deep occasional chair facing the television screen completed the furniture. It gave you plenty of opportunity to see the rose-colored pattern of the rug being repeated down a long distance to the desk.

Dwight had just arisen from behind the desk. He came forward, the black dressing gown hugging his stout frame. A diamond on his fourth finger, right hand, threw splinters of light in my eyes. Dwight's head was impressive, large and well-formed, a head you might expect to see on a statesman or a famed religious leader. The black-rimmed pince-nez perched on a long, high-bridged nose; the sun-bleached streak through his abundant dark hair, added to his air of distinction. Altogether, he was tall and well-built and impressive, except for the slight sullen down-droop of his small mouth which somehow spoiled the picture. He was perhaps forty-five years old.

"My name is Tocca," the captain began. The wallet opened and closed again. "Homicide, Chicago." We stood facing Dwight like a couple of boxers awaiting the lunge of an opponent.

"I'll say first of all, Captain," Dwight replied smoothly, "that you're out of jurisdiction. This is not Chicago."

"I don't think I'll have any trouble straightening that out," Tocca said firmly. "The police forces of Cook County are very co-operative, Mr. Dwight. So don't let it bother you."

Dwight shrugged. He walked slowly to his desk, drew a cigarette from a gleaming silver box and lit it with a heavy silver table lighter as he asked, "Why do the Chicago police allow newspapermen to follow them around, Captain?" He snapped off the lighter and glared at me down the room. "This man Harry

Diamond wrote a thing or two about my wife that I didn't care for."

"I'll ask the questions, Mr. Dwight," Tocca said easily. "I'm here concerning the murder of a business friend of yours—Al Asperito."

"Murder?" Dwight frowned.

Tocca nodded. "Earlier this evening. At his home."

"Captain," Dwight said, advancing down the room, "you're treading on dangerous ground when you accuse me of doing business with a criminal like Asperito. I happen to know he owns a good deal of slum property in this city, both on West Madison and in the colored district on the south side. My business is distilling, and it's completely legal."

Tocca smiled thinly. He walked over to the long table, brushed a finger across the polished top and looked for dust that wasn't there. "You had a meeting here last night, Mr. Dwight. In this room, at this table. *You* called that meeting."

Dwight had gone pale beneath his golden tan. He stood rigidly waiting, until Tocca had delivered enough of the story to make Dwight sure that he knew it all. "Now," Tocca said, "I think I'm safely off that dangerous ground you mentioned."

"No move has been taken!" Dwight replied. "We discussed the subject, that's all."

"But there's been a murder," Tocca shot back. "A murder meant to impress you and your other friends. The man who put the note on the table last night was apparently trying to demonstrate that it's dangerous—or fatal—to buck the syndicate." Tocca unwrapped a fresh cigar, got it going. "I'm not nosing into your business, Dwight, illegal or otherwise, much as I'd like to. I'm interested in who killed Asperito. If that happens to get tangled up in your business enterprises, I can't help it. Do I make myself clear?"

Dwight lowered himself into one of the chairs. He nodded, his eyes focusing on the table's smooth sheen.

"I want some facts about this meeting last night." And when Dwight looked up in protest, Tocca said sharply, "It may bear on the matter of the murder." Cigar smoke clouded the room as Tocca thought for a moment. "The lights went out last night for a minute or so, and it was impossible to see anything, according to Asperito. What time did the lights go out?"

"About. . . . I believe it was between ten-five and -fifteen. Somewhere in there, at least." Dwight's diamond clacked on the table top as he moved his fingers restlessly.

"The note," Tocca said. "I'd like to see it, if you have it."

"It's in my safe." Dwight rose and walked to his desk. He took down half a dozen books from a shelf at shoulder height behind the desk, then his back shielded the safe from sight. In a minute he returned with the paper. I saw a round black dial recessed at the rear of the book shelf. Tocca studied the note and I looked on over his shoulder. The paper was heavy bond that you could buy at any stationery store, and the pica type had no defects such as crooked letters that I could see.

Double-spaced, the note said: *Gentlemen, I am*

one of you sitting at this table. I represent the New York syndicate. We are going to organize the city for you on a more efficient basis. It will be safer for all of you if you co-operate. Tocca handed it to me when he had finished reading and I hastily copied the words on my pad that Tocca had returned.

Tocca rattled the paper. "Asperito said you passed this note around last night."

"That's correct," Dwight said. His mouth opened slightly as if he were ready to say more, then his lips clamped together.

"In that case," Tocca said, "the prints of every man at this table will be on the paper, so damned jumbled that they'll mean next to nothing." With a tiny exclamation of disgust, he slid the paper onto the table. "I'd like to use your phone." Tocca went to the desk at the other end and started dialing. I sat down in the occasional chair, getting a cigarette going. *Clack-clack* went Dwight's diamond against the table top.

"Hello, operator. Captain Mario Tocca, Chicago Homicide, speaking. Police business. Let me have the local power company." Tocca waited, chewing on his cigar. I suddenly realized that I felt cool, and for the first time I heard the whir of air conditioning. I had been too interested up to now to appreciate it.

Tocca repeated his name again, then asked, "Was there a power failure last night during the storm? Anything that would affect the home of William Dwight, on Sheridan Road?" He listened. "All right, thanks." He put down the phone and turned, smiling a Cheshire smile. "No power failure last night, Dwight. None at all. Where's the master switch for the lights in this place?"

"Out—out in the garage. On the stairway up to my chauffeur's apartment."

"Okay," Tocca said. "Then the lights were flipped out last night by somebody in this house." Dwight's face suddenly looked bleached.

CHAPTER V

"We've got that much cleared up," Tocca said briskly. He rubbed his hands and grinned in my direction, to show me, I suppose, that official police methods didn't bog down in bungling as they were so often portrayed as doing. "Now, who in the house last night had an opportunity to put out those lights? If it couldn't be done from this room, then our friend with the note had to have an accomplice. How about the woman that brought us in?"

"Helen?" Dwight said abstractedly. He seemed to have trouble bringing his mind to bear on the question. "Helen had last night off. It's her regular time."

"You said something about the chauffeur's apartment. You have a chauffeur?"

Dwight nodded. "Alex Noonan."

"Was he off last night, too?" Tocca asked cynically.

"He might have been. I told him I wouldn't be going out. I don't know what he did after that." I thought that the answer to that might hinge on whether or not Dwight himself was the seventh man. "Noonan should be in his rooms now," Dwight offered.

"You're nice and co-operative, Dwight," Tocca said. Dwight seemed to ignore the sarcasm implicit in the policeman's tone. "You're married, aren't you? Where was your wife last night?"

"Here. In the house."

"I want to talk to her, if she's home now."

"Look, Captain, do you have to drag her into this?"

Tocca's dark eyes blazed. "Who's dragging anybody in? I'm asking the questions, Dwight. If you can call her on the phone or send your maid for her, that'll be okay. We can talk here." He wandered to the television set and examined the different control knobs. Dwight leaned over the phone on the desk, and dialed a number. Tocca swiveled suddenly. "Tell her to come down. And that's *all!*"

Dwight scowled, but told his wife that he would like to see her in the den. He hung up again, hand clenched on the phone, glaring at Tocca who had resumed his examination of the television.

One of the study doors opened and Linda Dwight came one pace into the room. She wore a deep yellow lounging robe, drawn tightly around her body, and no make-up except the coral tint of her nails. The rather flat face seemed remarkably pretty with its lipstick and powder gone, and yet the eyes as they went swiftly around the room were a shade too calculating. "Bill . . . ?" she said as she saw her husband behind the desk.

Tocca stepped forward commandingly. "Mrs. Dwight, I'm Captain Tocca of Chicago Homicide." He glared down the length of the room at Dwight. "Wait outside, will you please?"

Dwight stalked out the door, after a reassuring pat on his wife's shoulder. Linda Dwight seemed puzzled, but not alarmed. She dug a pack of cigarettes from the pocket of her robe and lit one. As Tocca shut the door and she blew out the match, her eyes caught mine. "Well, well," she purred. "North Clark Street's answer to Walter Winchell."

"Hello, Mrs. Dwight," I said.

Tocca grinned. "So you two know each other, eh?" He faced the woman. "Mrs. Dwight, your boy-friend Asperito was murdered tonight."

"Watch that 'boy friend' business," she said, and I could see the skin tighten on her pale hands. "*Mur——?*" Only then did the meaning of Tocca's words strike her. She looked amazed, then she puffed out her breath in a wheezing laugh. "This is some sort of joke, isn't it?"

"No, it isn't," Tocca said flatly. "Al Asperito is dead."

"How——?"

"Let me ask the questions, please. You can sit down if you want to," he added. She remained standing. "Mrs. Dwight, you know your husband had a meeting in this house last night. Al Asperito was here, and a number of other men, none of them what you could call solid, exemplary citizens."

"There was a meeting," she said defensively. "Al came, and some others, yes. As for the rest, I don't know what you're talking about." Mrs. Dwight seemed not at all grief-stricken to hear that her recent escort was dead.

"Did your husband tell you anything about what went on at the meeting?"

"Why, no." She laughed. "I don't bother myself with such things, Captain."

"Did you bother yourself about the lights going out?" Tocca asked.

"Last night? No, should I have? I thought some lines might be down because of the rain."

"What time *did* the lights go out, Mrs. Dwight?" Tocca said sharply, leaning forward.

But Tocca couldn't throw her. She eyed him coolly, her breasts taut under the yellow robe. "That's easy to answer, Captain. When the lights came on, I looked at the clock on the table next to my bed. It was exactly twelve minutes after ten. I was in my room, reading."

"Had you been here all evening?" Tocca asked.

She nodded. "Helen can prove that. She was upstairs most of the evening. I didn't kill him, Captain. He wasn't worth it. He took me out, but a number of men have done that. I didn't need him for my— my meal ticket." The last words had a caustic sting.

Tocca sighed and looked at me. "Any questions you want to ask?" he said heavily. I could see that he had run out of questions. "Mrs. Dwight," I asked, walking toward her, "you might not have killed Asperito. How about your husband?"

"You've got a grubby mind, Diamond," she said venomously.

"Maybe I have. But say your husband got jealous of Asperito hanging around you, taking you out to night clubs? That ought to be motive enough for anyone."

"Bill isn't that kind of a romantic fool, Diamond," she bit out. "Ours is what you might call a business arrangement. That's public knowledge, so you won't cause any stir in your paper if you print it. As I say, Al

Asperito isn't—wasn't the first man who took me out after I married Bill. If Bill were the kind of man you think he is, you'd have a dozen murders, not just one."

"All right," I said. "Thanks." I was convinced that the line of questioning led nowhere. Tocca opened the door for Linda Dwight, telling her she could go, and he motioned for me to follow. Dwight started to speak to his wife until Tocca waved him off with a gesture. Glowering angrily, he watched Linda Dwight ascend the curving stairs, the yellow robe clinging tight over her hips. I felt sorry for William Dwight, if theirs was only a business arrangement.

Tocca told Dwight, "We'll go see your chauffeur now."

Dwight belted his robe more tightly around his middle. He led us down another short hall, through the kitchen and out into the back yard. A garage stood squarely at the end of the driveway, and beyond it I heard the lake hissing. Over the garage, a light burned in a window. Dwight led the way down a footpath, opened a door at the side of the garage and flicked a light switch. Halfway up the stairs he stopped and indicated one of two gray steel boxes attached to the outside wall. Tocca pulled it open. A large toggle switch was attached inside. "This turns out the lights all over the place?" Tocca asked. Dwight replied that it did. We went on up the stairs and Dwight knocked at the door at the top.

A man of about thirty-five, wearing suntans and a T-shirt, opened the door. A science-fiction magazine, with a brief-clad girl screaming silently in the clutches of a round green monster on the cover,

"Messenger?" Tocca snapped. "What sort of messenger?"

"One of those delivery services," Noonan replied. "There was two hundred bucks in a long yellow envelope, and this note telling me to turn out the lights by the main switch between ten and ten fifteen. For thirty seconds I was supposed to turn them out." Noonan scrubbed at his sweaty forehead with his right palm. "The note said something about my old lady getting hurt if I didn't. What the hell, Mr. Dwight, what could I do? Two hundred bucks for turning out some lights? It didn't seem like any big crime or anything."

Dwight nodded sympathetically. Tocca said, "Where's that note now?"

"I—I tore it up and flushed it down the john."

Tocca's mouth screwed to one side, exasperatedly. He asked Dwight, "When did you call your little meeting, Dwight? It has to be after you learned that O'Riordan died, but what time?"

Dwight's tan grew a shade darker. "I don't think that concerns——"

"Whether it concerns me or not is for me to decide. I know you don't like the idea of my thinking that a respectable citizen would dream up a scheme for organizing the rackets in the city, but Asperito's dead, and that meeting hooks up with his death. What time did you call?"

"I started calling around three. I reached Otto Schloss, last of all, somewhere between four-thirty and a quarter to five."

"Asperito?" Noonan bubbled. "Al Asperito? Is he dead?"

"Yeah," Tocca said flatly. "You make sure you don't step out of line any more, Noonan. I'll be wanting to talk to you some more in the next day or so. . . . Dwight, we're finished out here." Tocca stalked toward the stairs. I had a last glimpse of Alex Noonan hugging the science-fiction magazine to his chest as if it contained the wisdom to pull him out of the deep, dark hole that had caved in on top of him. Tocca walked straight back to the portico, opened the door of the squad car and started to climb in. Dwight stood by nervously as Tocca played with him, made him wait. Tocca settled himself in the front seat, and closed the door. He leaned out the window as I climbed in back.

"I want you downtown at headquarters tomorrow afternoon at one-thirty, Dwight," Tocca said. The driver clicked the headlights alive, and in their glow I saw Dwight nod, tight-lipped. The gears clashed and the driver backed the squad car down the drive, waited for a passing car at Sheridan, then backed out farther, swung across into the right-hand lane heading south.

"I didn't get anything," I said to Tocca. "Did you?"

"Ah, not much," he growled disgustedly. "Hey," he said to the driver abruptly, "take me to the Wilmette station. I want to clear things up there before we go back downtown."

"I haven't got anything worth printing, yet," I said.

"Now that's too bad." Tocca's temper was strained. "Well, I'll collect the five living witnesses to Dwight's little meeting and have them all downtown tomorrow. I'll put my money on one of them, Diamond."

"You've got five choices," I said tiredly. I leaned

back against the cushions, hot wind fanning the sweat on my forehead. My wrist watch said it was well after one o'clock. To Tocca I said, "I'll be at the meeting tomorrow afternoon, Captain."

"I damn well wish I could keep you out," Tocca said with feeling.

I leaned back and closed my eyes. We made a ten-minute stop at the Wilmette station house. Tocca came back and said, "Okay," to the driver and we started south again. It seemed no time at all before I was climbing out of the car at Sheridan and Lawrence and muttered my thanks.

Tocca's hand caught my arm from the open car window. Tired lines etched themselves around his mouth. "Remember, Diamond. You can do what you want, so long as you don't try to take our regular business away from us. We'll do the investigating. Keep that in mind."

"I'll keep that in mind," I lied. The car shot away from the curb and its tail lights dwindled down Sheridan, red eyes shrinking to pinpoints and then vanishing behind the oncoming headlight glare. I crossed Sheridan, angled across the vacant lot and walked up Lakeside. I needed the sack more than anything else.

But once stripped, with the fan going, I couldn't sleep. I got a beer out of the ice-box and lay drinking it. Al Asperito was dead. That one fact repeated itself in my mind. Tocca was fighting a battle against man's ancient foe, time, to keep the syndicate from moving in. The seventh man's plans were in the early stages now, but unless Tocca could get him quickly, the whole city might knuckle under. They had power, that was sure.

Back of him, the seventh man had unlimited money and information, and that could put a lot of advantage on his side, despite the fact that he worked alone. For instance, the business about Alex Noonan and the lights that went out at a certain time. The seventh man had gotten Dwight's call, and immediately put in a call of his own, threatening Noonan's mother. That presupposed a good deal of information, a research organization of the underworld that knew who had family connections to be exploited, and it included even cheap ex-convicts like Noonan, because no man could afford to be passed up since he might become valuable at some unexpected moment.

Then the seventh man sent his note to Noonan, plus money to insure the accomplishment of the task. And while the seventh man sat at Dwight's table in the den and the hot rain thudded down on the roof, Alex Noonan threw the switch. Out went the lights, a hand slid the typed note onto the table, the lights came on again, Al Asperito protested. And the machinery of murder hummed alive. . . .

. . . To end in Asperito, the little ex-hood, who'd been so worried about his character, then, at the last moment worrying only about the red flow of blood over his fingers. Devilish. And yet it was plausible, which made it all the worse.

The seventh man crayoned the message to tell me to stop connecting Dwight and Asperito. As a further inducement, he shot at me. Then I grappled with him in the darkness near Asperito's bungalow. A detached portion of my mind made me want to know the answer. But as I lay there drinking cold beer in the darkness, another part of my mind burned with red heat, because I wanted my own hands to have a part in shaping the end of the seventh man. And I knew that with each passing hour, it was becoming more and more impossible for me to pull out.

I drank the last of the beer, knowing death might be at the end of the road. I was going down that road, and the seventh man would be waiting at the end. He would learn his lesson.

Sleep came in a beery haze of anger.

CHAPTER VI

When I woke up at nine the next morning I felt gusts
of cooler air coming in through the windows. The curtains stood out at fitful intervals in a forty-five degree
angle from the wall, and the sheets felt a little dryer
than usual. All this aided in boosting my feeling of
well-being up a couple of notches. I actually felt cool
and dry at the end of my shower. Chilled orange
juice and my first cigarette both tasted delicious. I
walked over to the Broadway garage, handed the attendant my car keys and had a cup of coffee in Wal-
green's while they rescued my Chevvy from out front
at Asperito's. By quarter after ten I was on the Drive
going down town, thinking rambling Wordsworthian
thoughts about spring, although it was full summer
and I only deluded myself into thinking the season
was another, more pleasant one. Asperito's death
seemed an illusion, the bloodstains on his clutching
hands like the dapplings of a butterfly that dips and
wheels through a nightmare. By the time I took the
elevator up to my office, though, I had thought over
the previous night's happenings enough to realize
that my early-morning bounce by all rights should
have deflated itself by now. It had.

Nevertheless, I managed a grin as I entered the

office. Artie was at the typewriter again, while Rosemary sat next to the window, writing leisurely in a large spiral notebook. She glanced up and I had the embarrassing feeling that a small light akin to a glow had come into her eyes.

" 'Morning," I said, depositing my hat on a convenient chair.

Artie rested his elbows on the top of the typewriter and regarded me with a dour eye while he sucked on a thin-stemmed pipe. "Hi, Harry," Rosemary said, sounding almost carefree.

Artie continued to fix me with the evil eye. "What's wrong with you?" I said, lighting a cigarette.

"I think it's only fair that I should inform you," Artie said in a mock-serious voice, "that you had better start thinking up column material, p.d.q., as my father's old saying goes." Rosemary laughed brightly. I sat down behind the desk and examined my blank pad.

"The column's going to pot, eh?"

"That's approximately it, yes," Artie said. "Of course, you might say that the entertainment calendar dwindles as the heat increases, or——"

"He means you can't write about the ball game *every* day," Rosemary put in.

"Go to hell," I said politely to Artie.

"I will, if I get a by-line," said Artie. Rosemary's rippling laugh suddenly filled the room with pleasantness.

I settled myself behind the desk. "I have news," I said, "unfit to print. I expect Charlie Parnell or one of the other police beat boys has already picked it up." Rosemary's gaze focused on me, slightly worried. "Al Asperito was murdered last night."

"Great balls of fire!" Artie breathed.

Rosemary stood up quickly. "Harry! While you . . . ?"

I nodded. "Just before I got there. I spent the evening with Mario Tocca, the Homicide captain. The whole thing's a dilly of a yarn, but we can't print it. Or at least we aren't going to. But if it gets out that it happens to be my doing. . . ." I drew a finger across my neck.

"Wait a minute," Artie said, his brow knotting in a frown. "Are you trying to say that you're the boy responsible for squelching a good story?"

"That's exactly it," I said. "If you've got any loyalty to your employer, hold on to it. I've got a good reason." I could almost see my reason in black crayon, lettered on a windshield. I could feel it in a small lead slug resting in my palm, and in the blows of a killer fighting me beside a darkened house. "As far as this paper is concerned, we'll know no more than what Tocca releases to all of 'em."

Rosemary's hands were clasped tight. "Harry, I told you that Asperito would only get you into trouble."

"Relax," I said, stifling irritation. "Several other gentlemen around the town are in more trouble."

"There's something more behind this, eh?" Artie asked, settling himself in a hunched-over position on the window sill. "Something big, maybe? Behind just a plain murder?"

"It's not exactly a plain murder," I said, with a taste of last night's heat flat in my mouth. "But you're right, there is something big behind it. Very big. You keep your mouths clamped tight and I'll let you in on it." They promised. I knew that I could trust both of them, though I realized that I had never before been in a position to intrust them with anything this important. Still, I wanted to talk it out again in my own words. I got up, shut the office door and started in with my arrival at Asperito's, carrying it through the events at Dwight's home. Rosemary's attitude of concern deepened progressively with each word.

When I finished, Rosemary took a quick, jerky step toward the desk. I knew what was coming. I stood up and jabbed another cigarette into my mouth. Telling the story had released no tensions, nor straightened out any of the kinks. Instead the tension had pressure-cookered inside me and the telling had only acted as a valve to keep the anger from exploding.

"Harry," Rosemary said, "are you sure they don't think you had anything to do with killing him?"

"No, they don't think I had a thing to do with it," I said with some uncertainty, since I wasn't quite sure of Tocca's viewpoint on the matter. "Look," I said sharply, "I'm all right. I don't need lectures on how to behave myself. I've managed to stay out of trouble this far, and——" I stopped. Rosemary bit her lip and turned her head. Feeling like a louse, I touched her arm and mumbled, "I'm sorry, Rosemary."

"That's all right," she said, her shoulders lifting as she sighed and composed herself. "I was butting in." But I knew it was not all right, by any means.

"How about me buying you a cup of coffee in a couple of minutes?" I asked.

"That would be fine." She kept her head averted.

"You—you go fix your make-up and we'll drop downstairs. Okay?" Her eyes flashed her thanks for my releasing her. She left the office quickly, closing the door after her. I settled behind the desk again. Artie jumped off the window sill and came round in front of me.

"I've got a question," he said.

"If it's about my capacities for handling my own affairs, save it."

"No, no, it isn't that. I was just wondering, did you tell Tocca about that Tripp coming to see you?"

I felt as if a bucket of ice water had cascaded over me. I snapped my fingers. "By God!" I said.

"Aha!" he crowed. "Subconsciously suppressing evidence. You're thinking of yourself as the great detective, eh?"

"Bull!" I said. "I remember now what I told Tocca. I said, 'Asperito got in touch with me.' But I didn't tell him how."

"I don't exactly see how you could think at all, right after you found Asperito shot," Artie said seriously.

"You've got a point," I said. "It isn't as easy as it looks." But I felt a nasty inward laugh creep up, because I had something Tocca didn't have. It probably wasn't important, but it could be. I phoned up Maggie Hertzberg on the society desk.

"Hello, Harry," she rasped. "How's the hot-shot threat to husbands?"

"I've reformed," I said. "I'm not on the trail of Linda Dwight. What's the condition of her tie with her husband? She told me it was a business arrangement, but I wanted an objective opinion."

"She was telling the truth, more or less," Maggie replied. "I imagine there was some domestic interplay four or five years ago when they were first married."

"You sound like a professor. 'Domestic interplay,' my eye!"

"Now Harry, boy. Be good to an old lady. The interplay's all over. Linda Dwight has been out with numerous eager young men, at all the big places. That's been going on for the past two, three years. I don't think Dwight minds his wife having fun."

"You've got a bawdy mind," I said, "but thanks just the same."

I hung up as she started to tell me a joke about a new man in a lumber camp. I starred the memo concerning Fatsy Patsy Tripp and replaced the book in my shirt pocket.

The door opened and Rosemary came in. "All ready for that coffee," she said.

Artie returned to the typewriter as I walked to the door. "If I was a big columnist," Artie complained, "I'd stick to business."

"You stick to business and find me something to write about," I said as I followed Rosemary out the door again. "I'll give you ten bucks." Rosemary smiled at me as the elevator whisked us down, and I felt thankful for the motion required in walking, since it gave me something to concentrate upon, putting one foot before the other. I was afraid that my strategy was all too obvious, and when we were seated across from one another in the rattling, clicking near-noon interior of the drugstore, I was sure of it.

Rosemary poured a long stream of sugar into her black coffee and began stirring it. "You really didn't have to spend your money extravagantly, Mr. Diamond," she said. "Ten cents is a rather expensive bribe."

I gulped down some of my coffee. "I plead guilty," I said. I offered Rosemary a cigarette and lit it for her, feeling ninety per cent miserable. I had acted like a heel, then tried to remedy the damage, and I had been found out.

"For heaven's sake, don't frown so," Rosemary said. "I was only teasing."

"Well, I admit it. I lost my temper in the office."

"I can't blame you," she said.

"*What?*"

"I said I can't blame you." In my surprise I started to interrupt, but she kept me silent with a small shake of her head. "Let me say something that needs to be said, Harry." Her blue eyes had become entirely serious now, and her voice slipped a notch lower. "I know you get tired of my fussing over you. It's silly, it's old fashioned, and a man resents it."

"No——" I began.

"Don't try to deny it. As soon as I say some of the things I do, I know inside that I've made a fool of myself." Her chin lifted. " 'Rosemary,' I say to myself, 'you're a woman who's lived long enough to know how the modern world runs. Men, especially Harry, don't want a hen clucking over them. You're supposed to be bright and sophisticated and even a little immoral in what you say, but never let a man think you're trying to mother him or he'll shy away.' "

"That's ridiculous," I said. "You're not the motherly type. With your face and your figure. . . ."

"There! You see!" she exclaimed softly. "That's the modern man. You simply can't believe that a woman can be what I am. Harry, I can't believe it either, sometimes, but that's the way I am. Blame my parents, my upbringing, anything you want. No matter how I bother myself about it, I know I can't change, just as I know that I'm only being foolish when I act that way."

I inched my hand across the table and closed it on hers. The rich coffee aroma, the clatter of silver and the loud conversation of the fountain seemed to drift carelessly off into some middle distance. Our eyes stayed locked.

"I'll try to keep from losing my head," I said. "Honest to God I will, Rosemary."

"You can't change any more than I," she replied. Quickly then, with a slight tinge of embarrassed color in her cheeks, she disengaged her hand and swirled her coffee around in the cup, taking a long drink. "I only thought it would help to clear the air if I told you that I understood myself. Ordinarily, my natural instincts stay hidden where they belong most of the time. Since this Asperito business came up, I—I'm afraid I haven't been able to hold onto myself as well as I should have." The warm, flashing smile crossed her face again. "Here I am being deadly serious. You see? Right there I'm reverting to nineteen hundred, when this isn't nineteen hundred at all."

"Tell me something," I said, attempting to make a

joke of it. "Do you feel this way about every man?"

"That's a loaded and vicious question, Mr. Diamond."

"Well, do you?"

"No, I don't," she said softly. "And if you laugh, you can go straight to hell!"

I did laugh, and so did she. "That last was lifted bodily from the Modern Girl script," she admitted. "I was never cut out to be an actress."

"You seem to me to be cut out to be the nicest there is."

"Oh, no." She shook her head vigorously. "You wouldn't say that if you knew what I've been thinking." This time her hand sought mine, and I could feel the faint coldness of her palm. "Harry, this *is* dangerous, this whole business of your wanting to catch the seventh man. . . ."

Something stiffened inside me. "I explained how I felt to you and Artie."

"And you're still going after him? Knowing how dangerous it might be?"

I nodded doggedly. "Yes."

When the smile came to her lips again, it was the same as before. But the smile of her eyes seemed a screen, behind which I thought I saw worry lurking again. For once in our relationship I paused to think what prompted that worry, and arrived at the same answer I had arrived at before. But the difference came in my own emotions. How did I feel? Never once had I answered that question.

"Well, I'll try my darnedest to keep from being the Little Mother," Rosemary said, glancing down at her coffee. "I've finished, Harry."

How did I feel? Was my anger a shield? Was . . . ?

A sharp *brat-tat-tat* filled my ears. I turned my head, the mood broken. At the next counter a small boy was swinging a toy machine gun back and forth, making the sounds with his mouth. I stared into space and envisioned a man deep in leather and fur, still deeper in the steel heart of a fighter plane, amid the racketing death of a torn and smoke-trailed sky.

"What's wrong, Harry?" Rosemary asked.

"I was wondering," I said, almost to myself, "whether you liked to mother . . . your husband." The words had the miserable taste of gall on my tongue.

She seemed crestfallen. "Yes, I did, Harry." Then she was up from the booth and trying to smile. I paid the check, cursing myself for a jealous, angry fool, but the slender thread of the moment had broken and could not be retied.

In the lobby, Rosemary said, "Good-by, Harry. Thanks for the coffee." She turned and walked rapidly toward the elevators, as if she were afraid of herself and had to walk rapidly to get away.

When I left Rosemary my watch showed ten minutes after one. I got my car from under Michigan and drove to police headquarters, that squat pigeon-spattered building I'd only visited a few times during my so-called journalistic career, but never on an occasion as important as this. The desk sergeant directed me to the second floor. The five men sat nervously on benches along the wall, as if they were afraid to be seen speaking to one another.

I said a casual "Hello" to William Dwight. He muttered something for politeness' sake and went back to studying his fingernails. I scrutinized the five men for a second or two, knowing that the murderer of Al Asperito sat among them. With five pairs of eyes averted, intent on personal preparations for the ordeal with Tocca, I saw no hint of recognition. *One* of the five knew who I was. One of the five was the seventh man, and for a fraction of an instant the small of my back crawled.

My knock on Tocca's door was medium-polite. He said, "Come in," and I reminded myself that I had to be very observant.

Tocca sat in shirt sleeves behind his desk, studying a piece of paper with a number of black boxes drawn on it in India ink. I couldn't grasp the significance. I lowered myself into a chair and lit a cigarette. Tocca turned the paper sideways and studied it. I inhaled and said, "Is the big show ready to begin?"

Tocca gave a tight nod of his head.

"They're all sitting out there," I said, "like little girls at a dancing school, jumpy because they don't think they'll get to waltz." I eyed my glowing cigarette tip. "I guess, though, they'd rather sit it out, eh?"

"I wish that's *all* they were, girls in dancing school," Tocca said tonelessly, dropping the paper onto others cluttering the green blotting pad.

Tocca's cigar had gone out and he reached for matches in his wilting shirt pocket with a tired sigh. His hand, carrying the lighted match to his mouth, seemed arrested, like a slowed movie film; but that came from my own urge to know just how he was going to handle the little series of scenes that would soon be enacted in this plain, gritty efficient office. It struck me that Tocca could now play God to a lesser extent, controlling the lives of the men in the hall, the only difference being that God never made mistakes, while Tocca, as I could see in the worry-furrows on his forehead, was only too conscious that he was fallible.

Tocca frowned briefly at the India-inked paper on his desk. I reached out and took the paper and stared at it. Drawn along its length was a long rectangle, and the word "table" had been printed inside the thick black boundaries. Below this were six smaller squares, numbered from left to right. It obviously was the table arrangement of the meeting at Dwight's home, the night the seventh man slid his note out during the darkness, to begin the murder chain.

I handed the paper back. Tocca uncapped his fountain pen and laid it on top of the elaborate diagram and, rising with a resigned sigh, walked toward the door. "Hey," I said. "What's the picture for?"

He could hardly conceal his weary leer of triumph. "Wait and see." Tocca opened the door and leaned out. "Mr. Heinz, will you come in please?" I got my own writing materials propped on my knee as the bookie and policy boss came into the office. Tocca closed the door. "Have a seat, Mr. Heinz," he said.

Milo Heinz was short and slender; he wore a light blue jacket and matching slacks, dapperly fitting his frame. A bland, ordinary face topped by rust-colored thinning hair. He, like the other four I had seen ranged along the benches, was well over forty. He laced his fingers firmly over his stomach and regarded Tocca with mild indifference.

"I hope you understand the nature of this investigation, Mr. Heinz," Tocca said, with a ponderous enunciation that impressed nobody.

"It's an investigation intended to uncover the murderer of Al Asperito," he said with just a trace of a lisp. "Isn't that correct?" Without waiting for an answer, he said with placid assurance, "The lieutenant who talked to all five of us in the room down the hall explained things rather carefully."

He had glanced in my direction, and immediately away, when he came in. Perhaps *he* was the one. I had a peculiar feeling of uneasiness, coupled with a strong upsurge of anger, the moment he stepped into the office. For a precise mocking voice had spoken in my thoughts only a moment before: He will be clever, and you will never be able to tell from looking at him. His eyes will never show the shrewdness behind . . .

"I'm glad you have everything clear," Tocca replied. "You understand that I'm not investigating your business activities, much as I'd like to." Heinz matched Tocca's faint glower with a bland grimace of world-weariness.

"My business is pretty damned dull, Captain," he replied smoothly. "You'd be a fool to waste your time investigating that." The word *fool* was pronounced with a whisper as soft as an echo of wind, so intoned that it could not be mistaken for anything but an impersonal term, and yet mockery lay deep underneath.

"Then we'll take it for granted that I know what went on at William Dwight's home two nights ago,"

Tocca said heavily. "We'll save ourselves a lot of time if you don't try to deny such a meeting."

Heinz nodded agreement. Tocca took down Heinz's full name and address on a separate sheet of paper, then handed him the inked diagram. "This is a plan of the table in Mr. Dwight's study," he explained patiently. "I'd like you to tell me where you were sitting at the meeting."

"That's easy," Heinz replied affably. "I was here on the left, on the end. The box you've marked number one."

Tocca extended his hand and Heinz returned the paper. Even as I wrote into the notebook, I frowned, not quite sure of what he was trying to do. Tocca wrote the name of Heinz in box number one. "Now, Mr. Heinz," he said, "I'd like you to tell me where the other gentlemen were sitting that night."

Heinz frowned. He brushed his forehead with his palm and shook his head. "I'm afraid my memory's rather poor . . ."

"It's important that you remember," Tocca said with mild unpleasantness.

Heinz laughed gently. "My memory is—" he began again.

Tocca cut him off sharply. "Who was on your right?"

"I believe it was Bill Dwight. Yes, I'm sure of *that*, at least."

"And beyond Dwight?"

"I—I believe Roy Roblein was sitting to Bill's right."

"Beyond Roblein?"

"Jake Bushnell."

"Asperito next, by any chance?"

"Yes, I believe so."

"And Otto Schloss last?"

Heinz raised his palms upward. "I can't be quite sure, but I think that was the arrangement." His eyes blazed with open mockery at Tocca now, because he knew the diagram strategy was not routine, only what he would class as amateur theory.

Tocca's pen moved busily for a moment. "All right, Mr. Heinz. Now. Where were you between nine and ten last night? Or more specifically, at approximately twenty-five after nine?"

"I was in my apartment."

"Are you married, Mr. Heinz?"

"No, I am not."

"What were you doing at that time?"

"I was watching television," Heinz replied without hesitation. "It was an old film. The name of the picture was *South Seas Siren,* in case you're interested."

"That's all you were doing, watching television?" Tocca asked. His voice had grown heavier, a trifle more insistent.

"I was also working on some papers at the time."

"What sort of papers were they?"

"Captain," Heinz said, all trace of humor vanished, "you are not investigating my business."

Tocca's eyes locked with his for a moment and then Tocca glanced away, harried. "Any substantiation for your story?"

Heinz languidly lifted one shoulder. "None, I'm afraid."

"That'll be all. Send in Mr. Dwight on your way out."

Heinz rose and walked to the door. As his hand fastened on the knob, Tocca spoke. "What was your reaction to the syndicate announcement, Mr. Heinz?" he asked gently.

Not a muscle in Heinz's pale face stirred for a moment, and then a tiny quirk lifted the left-hand corner of his mouth. "I came to no decision, Captain," he said. "My policy is what is known as watchful waiting."

"That's all," Tocca said flatly. Heinz, composed and calm, left the office.

Tocca had time for no words with me, only a slightly frantic casting of his eyes in my direction. William Dwight entered the office, wearing a faultlessly tailored Palm Beach suit and a colorful tie. Dwight seemed at ease, and there was little tension between him and Tocca. They had come to a rough working understanding the night before. Tocca dispensed with the name-and-address business and offered Dwight the diagram. Dwight had no trouble at all remembering who had sat where. Tocca wrote Dwight's name in box number two. He corroborated Heinz's arrangement.

In the rest of the interviews, the arrangement never varied. Despite different degrees of recall, all five of the men agreed as to the seating positions. Milo Heinz's breakdown had been correct, but in spite of the tally, I did not understand until the last of them had gone what Tocca had intended when he first produced the chart.

"Tell me, Mr. Dwight," Tocca said. "Where were you at nine-thirty last night?"

"In my study," Dwight replied, seated near the edge of his chair, but stiff-shouldered as befitted a man of his dignity. His fingers were fastened firmly on the band of his Panama, but not with any nervous pressure. "I spent the evening reading," he added.

"Were you at home all evening?"

He thought a moment. "Yes. I ate dinner with Linda—Mrs. Dwight."

"What time was that?"

"Around seven or seven-fifteen. Then I went to the study, and I read until you and Mr. Diamond arrived."

"Anyone come into the study during that time?"

"No, no one."

Since Tocca had talked with Dwight the evening before, he evidently saw no reason for prolonging the conversation. But he asked the question about reaction to the syndicate note when Dwight reached the door. Dwight frowned thoughtfully for a moment before he answered, a dignified man who could not help but impress.

"I thought that the only possible course of action was one of consideration. Hasty decisions would not get us anywhere." Dwight's voice rose smoothly. "That is, I *would* have recommended consideration, Captain, had there really been a meeting at all." Dwight settled his hat on his head with a defiant snap of his wrist, designed to re-emphasize his strict insistence upon legal protocol. "May I go now, Captain?" he said heavily.

Tocca nodded and chewed the cigar furiously. "Send in Roy Roblein."

Roy Roblein, who dealt in women. He was a tall, lanky wild-haired giant of a man whose slacks and sport coat looked too heavy for the season, badly pressed and too short at wrists and ankles. His lean face had a rumpled, harassed look as he strode awkwardly into the office. He sat practically all the way down on his spine, his legs extending at an uneasy angle. His blue eyes jumped from wall to wall, floor to ceiling, my face to Tocca's, like balls in a pinball machine. He gave his name and address in a heavy rasping voice and went through the diagram routine. Every minute or so he would smile, crookedly and at nothing in particular, then lapse into rumpled embarrassment.

"Where were you last night?" Tocca repeated his question.

Roblein turned his nervous grin on and off again, massaged his jaw and shifted around in his chair. "Why, I guess right then I was out at the Voodoo Club." I watched his thin, muscular fingers that looked steel-strong, and had to admit that his smile had a twisted sort of charm. It was easy enough to imagine him ruling his women. If the smile failed, the lean fingers could break bone.

When Tocca asked for it, Roblein gave the location of the club: on Bryn Mawr near the Howard-Loop El station.

"Were you alone?"

"No, Captain, I had some girls with me."

"What are their names?"

"Flo Wrightsell, Hazel Coombs, Betty Marlo, and Jill somebody. I—ah—can't think of the last name."

"Addresses?"

The embarrassed shy-boy smile grew deeper and Roblein's eyes roved frantically. "Why, captain, I don't exactly know their addresses right offhand, but I . . . Well, if you'll let me go back to my agency, I can get the addresses out of the files. They're models," he finished lamely.

Be careful, I said to myself. They're fooling you, they're all in a dirty underground business, and they know it. It might be this one. . . .

Tocca tapped his fountain pen on the desk blotter. Big Roy shifted jerkily in his seat, drawing in his left leg, then extending it. He combed his fingers through his thick crest of hair and took to massaging his cheek again. At last Tocca asked, "How about the syndicate proposal?"

Roblein's grin was ragged, his laugh more like a wheeze accompanied by a twitching spasm of the shoulders. "How do you mean, how about it? You mean what did I think about it?"

"Yes," Tocca said evenly.

"Well, Captain, I figured the way Mr. Dwight did, it was too soon to decide anything. Personally"— he frowned slightly—"I'd want to stay in business for myself, but it'd be tough against the syndicate, and I don't personally know whether or not I'd like to buck them." A flicker of fear seemed to light his blue eyes for a moment, then it vanished. He twisted himself around in the chair, looking like a scarecrow whose crosspiece had been stolen.

"I'm through with you," Tocca said, scowling at his cigar. "Get out."

"Sure, Captain." Roblein struggled lazily to his feet and stood, dry-washing his hands nervously. His heavy-lidded eyes flicked downward. "I was sorry to hear about Asperito. . . . He was a nice guy."

"You're all nice guys, aren't you?" Tocca said, biting down on his cigar and meeting Roblein's gaze with flinty anger.

"Maybe not your kind," Roblein replied softly. He ambled toward the door, his shoulders sagging a bit, and I sensed somehow that he was genuinely afraid of the syndicate. But a moment later I figured he was an actor, just like all of them. He merely mumbled when Tocca told him to send Jake Bushnell in.

In the brief interlude of peace, I glanced at Tocca. "They do treat this syndicate business as if it's a game, don't they?" I said.

"The goddam bums!" Tocca said vehemently. "They're so damned afraid of getting their rights violated!"

The door opened with a vibration of force and Jake Bushnell stood there. Jake Bushnell, the dope-dealer, a thick-faced man with hard piles of bunched muscles around his shoulders. His clothes were in bad taste and his heavy, faintly bluish lips shone damply. He gazed at Tocca with a rather dull-witted look, but his eyes were small malignant points of wariness, sunk into mounds of thick flesh. The name, the address, the chart, with all of Bushnell's replies curt and belligerent. He talked with the forced boldness of the inner coward.

"Al Asperito was murdered last night at nine-thirty or thereabouts . . ." Tocca began.

"He shot off his mouth at Dwight's," Bushnell growled back from where he sat, rising like a granite block out of the chair. "He was too damned quick and too damned wise." Bushnell shoved a cigarette in between his pendulous lips and lit it with rock-steady hard tubes of fingers.

"You thought the syndicate should move, didn't you?" Tocca asked, eyes on the blotter.

Bushnell exhibited a look of blank surprise, then scowled. "What if I did? I've got brains enough to figure out what's coming. I don't care if you are a cop and I'm on the other side. I know what the score is. It *isn't* a shooting match on the street, with armies of mugs blasting at each other." Bushnell snorted. "It's quick and personal, like with Al. I say be smart!"

"Are you scared?" Tocca said, looking at Bushnell.

Bushnell rocketed massively out of the chair, fingers fisted. "I don't have to listen to questions like that. You've got no business asking them, and your own lieutenant damn well said you didn't. So ask the right ones and get it over with, or else shut up and let me get out of here." Bushnell was fairly shaking with anger.

"This isn't your office," Tocca breathed with murderous softness. "This is police headquarters. Watch your language."

Bushnell sat down in the chair with a disgusted exclamation, folded his arms and stuck his jaw forward. Tocca studied the sheet of paper on which he had written the various alibis.

"Where were you at nine-thirty last night?"

"The Shubert Theater," Bushnell replied loudly, "in the middle of act one of *Golden Town*. Like to know what it was all about?" His voice rose a notch. "Maybe I can find the ticket stubs if you want to look at them."

Tocca's face darkened with submerged wrath. He fought for control, dueling across the desk with this loud, small-minded rock of a man filling the chair opposite. "Were you alone?" Tocca's voice almost quivered.

"No, I was with a woman. Rita Ray."

"What does she do for a living?" Tocca asked sourly.

"She used to be a model." The cynicism grew in Tocca's eyes, remembering Roblein's party of friends, until Bushnell volunteered the name of a large Loop department store, as well as Rita Ray's address on the near north side. Bushnell's voice had sunk as if he had checked his lumbering temper. Tocca dismissed him and he smirked openly in triumph. With a wild jerk he tore the door open and whirled, his shoulders nearly touching the wood on either side.

"I'm not scared of the cops," Bushnell bit out harshly. "I'm not afraid of that jerk, Quinn, either, but I've got sense enough to know what the smart thing is. You'd be better off if you knew what the smart thing was. You'd be a lot better off." With a defiant cock to his shoulders, he vanished in the hall, and I thought I heard a laugh rasping against the walls.

I studied the blurs of words I had written. All of them were actors, but which had the consummate skill?

The last of the group appeared in the doorway. "I

am Otto Schloss," he said, not defiantly, yet not with humility either. I looked up as he closed the door and the stifling air closed in upon us once more.

"Sit down, Mr. Schloss," Tocca said.

"*Danke,*" replied Schloss.

He wore an old-fashioned black suit that looked insufferably heavy. His cheeks had a glow of reddish health on them, his hair radiated crookedly outward from around his skull, and his off-white mustache hung down over the corners of his mouth. He looked spaniel-sad, but his hoods, I knew, could be ruthless. He looked more like the proprietor of an antique shop than a man from the fringes of the law. At the moment he was gravely solemn.

"The lieutenant explained . . . ?" Tocca said with the repetitive tiredness evident in every syllable.

"*Ja,* yes, he did. I am sorry that *Herr* Asperito is dead."

"So are we," Tocca said inanely. He completed the diagram business rapidly and then asked Otto Schloss for his alibi. Otto Schloss became apoplectic. The *Ach, Gott*'s and the *Du bist ein*'s flowed in guttural torrents from his writhing lips. Tocca waved his arms up and down and began to shout. "Wait a minute, Mr. Schloss. Wait a minute!"

Schloss' cheeks burned fiery scarlet. "I will not stand an accusation! I had no part in the killing of Asperito!" he said loudly.

"Nobody said you did. I'm not accusing you."

"What?" Schloss seemed taken aback.

"I have to ask you where you were last night," Tocca explained patiently, "because all the men present at Mr. Dwight's home are naturally suspects. I'm making no accusations."

Schloss studied his black-clad knees for a moment and then his white head bobbed. His voice when he spoke had softened a good deal. *"Bitte, es tut mir . . ."* With a sheepish smile and what actually seemed to be a blush instead of the cheeky red of anger, he shook his head. "Forgive me. When I get excited, I forget myself and speak *Deutsch,* German. Last evening . . . let me see . . . I was at home. I believe I went to sleep at somewhere near seven-thirty."

I was too tired to laugh at that.

"Are you married, Mr. Schloss?" Tocca droned.

"Yes, I am. That is, I was. I am a widower. Kätchen has been gone, oh, eighteen years now. I have no one else." With a forward-leaning motion he placed his well-manicured hands on the edge of the desk. "Forgive me, please, *Herr Kapitan,* for my outburst. The police of this country, I should realize, do not make such accusations. It is only that—that I lost my head, as you say it." He sat back with a childish smile of innocence.

My head was swimming from the heat, but more so from the whirlpools of unanswerable questions that went round and round inside the walls of my skull. I had seen no reactions I wanted to see. Each of the five men noticed me when he came in, but the main concern was with Tocca, or such was the act. Lord, I was sick of thinking about actors and acting. Otto Schloss remained noncommittal concerning his reaction to the syndicate ultimatum. Still murmuring apologies, he shuffled from the office, placing his black hat precisely on his white hair.

The final close of the door was the sound of salvation for the weary.

I lit a cigarette, tasting brass in my mouth. Tocca slumped in a frozen pose over the blotter, but in the muggy air of the small office I could almost feel the tense boiling murder-urge raging in his blood. From his lips came a weak, curious laugh. "Aren't they the damnedest bunch?" he said, the smile sickly upon his mouth.

I reached across for the filled-in diagram. Tocca relit his dead cigar and squinted questioningly through the fumes, asking me with his eyebrows what I thought of it. I shrugged and sailed the paper back onto the desk. "If it proves anything, you'll have to explain it to me."

Tocca loudly swiveled his chair a half turn to the right. "It proves exactly nothing. It proves what I thought right after I heard what Asperito told you." He snorted with a derisive sound. "Asperito had a good memory. The order in which I called them in was the order Asperito gave you. I thought I'd check and find out who sat where." One hand lifted and waved at me. "I had the idea that one of them, one of the five, might have a different story about where he sat the other night. I wanted to catch just one of them making a slip! Just a little slip, so long as it was something to go on!"

"Would it have made much difference if one of them had slipped?" I asked.

"No, I guess not," he admitted glumly. He sat up

straight and the chair protested. "I'm scared, Diamond. I'm scared I can't handle this thing right."

His eyes begged for assistance, for inspiration. And at the same time, they warned me to forget what I had just heard.

He sighed loudly and tapped a finger on the diagram. "This thing doesn't help one bit. There wasn't one variation. Not one little slip." His finger moved into box number one. "Heinz. Dwight in the second chair. Then Roy Roblein. Four, Jake Bushnell. Five, the dead man, and Otto Schloss the last one. Left to right."

The walls of the room seemed to close in tight on us. My insides roared with submerged anger, because the one I wanted had been less than three feet away from me, and I knew it and did not know it at the same time. The hate-knife's edge was fire-tempered and growing keener.

"How about the alibis?" I asked.

Tocca ran his finger down the paper. "Not much," he said dejectedly. "Look at Roblein, for instance. Four women. All of whom I'd be willing to bet are high-priced dames, any of whom wouldn't mind perjuring themselves as a favor to Big Roy." The bitterness flowed like a dark river in his speech. He was trapped within the limits of the very law he upheld, while Dwight and his associates could use lies and deception whenever they pleased.

"Bushnell!" Tocca said. "The Shubert Theater! The same as Heinz's television story. Somebody tells him what the show's about, and we're supposed to believe his story's true because it's too simple to be other-

wise. Diamond," he said with sudden fierceness, "do
you see what I mean? Every one of them could have
done it. Where men like this are concerned, there *is*
no airtight alibi. There never is anyway, not really.
Every one of the five could have committed the murder."

I nodded again.

"And that Schloss!" Tocca said wrathfully. "He
looks like an old man who ought to sit in the park
and feed the pigeons! And he controls the hoods in
this town. *Controls* them! A regular employment
agency. Diamond, the days of simple-minded crim-
inals are over."

"And that's what makes it so tough, eh?" I said.

Tocca rolled the cigar around in his mouth, all the
energy drained out of him. He could vent his rage to
me over the paradox of men like Dwight and Otto
Schloss, but when he faced them in person he knew
he had a tough job on his hands, far tougher than he
felt equipped to handle. I felt sorry for him. A man
in his line of work couldn't be blamed for blustering.

"In your opinion," I said slowly, "which one of
the five is the most likely candidate for the role of
the seventh man?"

Tocca folded his hands in front of him on the desk.
"That's hard to say. I'd pick Dwight or Bushnell.
Dwight because of the jealousy angle, Asperito and
his wife. Bushnell because he wanted to give in to
the syndicate right away. Both may be wrong. Dwight
may not give a damn about who his wife plays
around with, and the woman's story fits that. Bushnell may just be plain yellow, and I'd be willing to
accept that, too." The next sigh came out longer, and

more desperate. "All of them could have killed Asperito. All, or any one. They're tough men, underneath the particular front they keep up. They're vicious, and they've got power behind them." His dark eyes looked up from the desk, desperation beginning to show in them. "Well, I'll check everywhere I possibly can."

I left him fondling the diagram he had made, staring at it as a child stares at a new toy he cannot quite comprehend.

CHAPTER VII

I drove slowly back to the boulevard with coolish air fanning my face. One by one I turned the alibis over in my mind, arriving at the conclusion that I had gained exactly one worth-while lead from what Tocca had told me. Roy Roblein had the corroboration of four, but Jake Bushnell had only the corroboration of one. A name stuck in my mind in connection with Bushnell's story, the name Rita Ray. I decided to go see her, because the entire affair had gotten hold of me with far more than curiosity. Perhaps Rita Ray would lead me to the seventh man, the man who so badly needed a violent lesson. Sitting in an air-conditioned restaurant over cheeseburgers and coffee, I felt the anger simmer low inside my belly. Mario Tocca would be following a number of other leads that might produce information. I'd try Rita Ray on my own.

The telephone book in the lobby of our building produced an address on the near north side. I pushed my hat far back on my head to get the benefit of the breeze and went under Michigan to retrieve my car. Already the breeze was filling itself with wet heat, and clouds like gray cotton tufts blew across the sky. The tempo of life slowed again to humid weariness, and by the time I turned north into the Michigan traffic flow from Chicago Avenue, hot drops of rain dappled the windshield. Steam rose from the pavement in hissing gray ropes, and drivers began to lean aggressively on their horns. The respite had not lasted for long, and the nerve-fraying lady of Chicago summer was back doing her time-worn act. With the rain and the heat came oppression again, and the sluggish stirrings of restlessness. The weather reminded me of the syndicate, with the smothering process of the latter yet to come, but more ominous because of it.

The near north side, rows of once-rich brownstones, showed its true grime-streaked face in the hot drizzle. The giants of Chicago had moved on to the north, leaving only the hulls of the early Gold Coast grandeur. Stunted trees caught the rain on seared dusty leaves. A miniature theater marquee displayed an *avant garde* foreign film next to a restaurant where bloated old men ate soup with their hats on—an area no longer respectable and not yet slum. Rita Ray lived a block from Dearborn, on a north-south street where the buildings on opposite sides seemed to lean toward each other for protection. I found her building the same as the others, with yellowed lace curtains in the windows and a small white cardboard sign stuck in the corner of the bay. This particular sign announced: MME. IRENA, PHRENOLOGIST.

I stepped into the hallway, filled with ancient odors of dust and wood. The mailboxes were new and brass-shining, three of them. Rita Ray had the apartment on the third floor. I climbed the steps slowly, as if the age of the building had infected me the moment I stepped in the door. The hall ceilings were high and gloomy, and the doors had the tallness of an earlier generation. The third-floor apartment presented two doors, so I picked the one with the white card thumbtacked to it. Beyond the door I could hear music that I recognized as Stan Kenton. I knocked and waited, listening to the jarring muffled sounds of music set against the tomb silence.

I heard no footsteps. Without warning a voice said, "Yes?"

"Miss Ray? I'd like to speak to you for a moment. I'm Harry Diamond."

A short silence. I decided that at least she read the newspapers, because the door opened quickly and the voice said, "The newspaper columnist?"

"That's right," I said. It took me a moment to realize that the voice came from a body, but she was there, framed in gloom. I had hoped for an apartment with some light and life to it, but it had been a foolish hope. She stepped back out of the way, a tiny frown puckering her forehead, and I noticed a hardening of the face, a quick readiness for trouble that came from living in the middle of this dead jungle.

I stepped into the apartment and the music grew louder. The flat dry scent of a perfume drifted into my nostrils. The room was large, seeming to recede endlessly into that unnatural dimness the building favored. Light filtered thinly down, but the main source of illumination was a two-inch slit between the window curtains. Rita Ray made small talk, offering me a chair. I sat directly in line with the slit of light, but she curled her legs under her on an old but comfortable-looking sofa close to the wall, so that I could not make her out quite clearly. All the furniture was old, except the radio-phonograph console from which the music blared with subdued fury. Two abstract pieces of wire sculpturing rotated slowly from the ceiling.

I hardly had any impression of Rita Ray at all. She wore a medium-sheer blouse over her slender, almost bony figure, and through it I could see the dark dappling of freckles on her arms. Black slacks encased her long legs, and her russet hair was bound up in a dark blue turban. Her face, a pale oval in the gloom, wore a heavy coating of make-up. The eyes remained black circles, the pupils invisible. The only splash of color on the small-breasted severity of her was the bleeding-wound garishness of heavily applied lipstick.

She spoke with a harshness in her voice that modeling-school elocution could not quite erase. "I'm afraid I can't imagine why you would want to see me, Mr. Diamond. I read your column every day, of course, but I'm only a model, and models don't make interesting reading unless they're getting married to someone wealthy, or get in the movies."

She reached for a cigarette from a black enameled box on a coffee table and self-consciously tapped it on the back of her hand. I heard the distant sound of falling rain, like the tears of lonely people who had lived out their empty lives in this haunted building. I debated the prospect of giving her a line about an interview and decided against it.

"Miss Ray," I said, "I wonder if you could give me some information."

"About modeling?" The laugh came false and forced, designed to impress.

"No, not about modeling. About Jake Bushnell." Her shoulders and her narrow breasts lifted defensively. "I understand you were at the Shubert Theater with him last night."

"Yes, I was. What difference does it make?"

"I'm—I'm afraid I can't tell you that." I felt that I had worked myself into a trap. "It's in connection with police business," I finished.

"Police?" She bent forward. I kept quiet. "Are you a friend of Jake's?"

"I know him," I said.

"We had dinner here last night, and went to the theater and came back here for a drink. I'd like to know what connection that has with the police."

I sweated for a moment. "Did Jake leave the theater any time last night?"

She unfolded her legs swiftly and stood up. "I think you'd better get out of here, Mr. Diamond. I don't understand this, but I don't like it, either. If there's anything the police want to know, they can ask me." She walked quickly to the door and pulled it open. A bright trumpet passage whirled up and down from the phonograph like the surging of hatred. I was on my feet and at the door almost as rapidly as she was, because I had realized that I could get nothing that would make any difference. I thanked her, but the gesture didn't change the stark, bony anger on her hungry features. The door whipped shut with a sharp bang. I walked slowly down the stairs, wondering suddenly if she had been afraid. The thought was gratifying but unfounded. I resettled my hat on my head and walked out.

I saw the thickset man striding determinedly up the porch steps, coat open to display his rumpled white shirt. I knew him. Duffy, a Homicide lieutenant. It seemed that I had timed this whole thing wrong. He reached the porch, saw me and scowled. "Diamond, what are you doing here?"

"Looking around," I said.

He wasn't fooled. "Tocca told me you had something to do with this Asperito business. He said you were kind of nosey, too. You know better than to fool around with stuff like this." He stabbed my chest with a thick forefinger and his eyes held menace. "Stay out of police business, Diamond." The words came out with a savage bite. He took his finger away. Wet, rumpled and angry, he passed on into the building.

I hurried for my car, and the slanting rain turned the buildings to a row of windowed tombstones.

I parked under Michigan and hurried up the long stairs through the steady gray downpour. On an inter-building phone in the lobby I called Charlie Parnell's desk and was told that he'd gone. I had one more bit of information I wanted to follow out to the end, and Charlie would have to give me some assistance on the details. Scowling, I put a cigarette between my lips and turned to leave the booth. My eyes flicked down for a moment while I brought flame to the tip of the cigarette, and when I raised them again, I saw Charlie Parnell across the lobby, behind the long glinting plate glass window of the drugstore.

I slid into the vacant stool beside Charlie and said hello. His eyes lifted from the brown pool of creamed coffee, and his gaze sparkled with irritation. "God *damn* you!" he said gently.

I ordered a lemonade. "Did I interrupt the philosophizing?"

"I was trying to find some elements of pragmatism in early American Puritan idealism," he said to the coffee. Behind the flat-planed glasses that reflected fluorescent ceiling light, his eyes swung to me. "Laugh, Diamond, and I throw the bloody coffee all over you."

I laughed softly, but he didn't throw the coffee. "I need help, Charlie."

His eyes narrowed. "Messing where you don't belong?"

"You don't need to moralize over what I'm doing. I've got a bug, Charlie. The bug makes me mad. I want you to listen to things you hear about what's going on in this town, crime-wise. The bug has to be fed."

Charlie swirled his coffee around. I lifted the lemonade, drank, and watched Charlie carefully over the white top of the paper cup. "Bugs," Charlie said in a low tone, "can be dangerous things. A bug causes malaria, doesn't it? People die from malaria." His eyes locked with mine and I said nothing. At last he raised his left hand in the peace sign. "You want information. I won't moralize. I keep my ears open, Harry. You can have whatever I've got."

"Thanks. Now one more thing—that Pat Tripp. Where does he hang out?"

"*You're crazy, Harry!*" he said with soft violence. "You're not a cop, damn you, and . . . " Again our eyes met, and flickering movement came from behind his glasses. The sigh whispered out of his mouth like a sad wind. "Okay. I'll shut up. I'll let you stick that stupid neck out as far as you want. You go over on West Madison and try the Hollywood, or other bars around there. I can't guarantee that you'll find Fatsy Patsy, because even my dope can go stale."

I left Charlie pondering the infinity in the bottom of his coffee cup and took the elevator up to my office. Rosemary greeted me with a restrained hello, lips drawn tight together, and she tapped quickly out of the office on spiked heels. Artie took his pipe out of his mouth.

"You ought to be grateful. She's so scared you may get hurt, she won't even look at you. You've got the stuff I wish I had." He grinned wryly.

"Artie, you want to write my column for me?"

"What?" He came up out of the chair beaming. "Hell yes, you know I'd——"

I waved him silent, knuckling my eyes to get rid of a weariness that didn't come from lack of sleep. I had gone deep enough into the affairs of the seventh man to know that I had to find him, tear the mask from his face before I could start working efficiently again. "You'll get a full by-line when I go on my vacation in September," I told him. His grin showed me that he was willing. I outlined a few points to be covered in the forthcoming columns, and had just wound up when the phone rang. Artie reached out, lifted it, listened, then handed it to me. The grin had turned wry. I cupped a palm over the mouthpiece. "What is it?" I asked.

"I think you're gonna get torn, boss," Artie said.

I said hello, and the voice came at the other end as a minor relief from tension. "Tocca, Diamond. Duffy saw you out at the Ray girl's apartment. What were you doing there?" The words came flat, demanding, insistent.

"I told Duffy I was only looking around."

"The Ray girl said you asked her questions," Tocca barked.

"But I didn't get anything," I shot back, inwardly rankled.

"Whether you got anything or not, we aren't considering," Tocca replied freezingly. "You may have me over a barrel, Diamond, but I told you that I wouldn't allow any interference with police routine." I sensed that this speech was mainly bluff, delivered because Tocca felt he was duty-bound to do exactly this. The next words came widely spaced, punched out with the fury of rifle reports. "Is that plain?"

"Sure," I said affably.

"Good-by." A minor explosion went off when he slammed down his end of the phone. I grinned a little sourly and shook my head. I felt good on the way down in the elevator, because I had the lead on Tripp. Tocca couldn't claim I was interfering with police routine when he knew nothing of Tripp's visit, could he? As I drove through the Loop, I reminded myself that I was a low-grade of rationalizer, but that didn't make me feel bad at all.

Eliot's Wasteland begins west of the river on that saloon-infested street where a Ph.D. makes you no better than the next man unless you happen to have the price of a drink. I parked just beyond the dirty bulk of the Northwestern terminal, locked both doors of my car and set out along the pavement of West Madison through the slacked-off rain. A group of men queued in front of a flophouse, identical figures in dirty overcoats and caps. Dull unfeeling eyes followed me as I walked. Old men broke from the cover of bar doorways to hold out leathered palms, and the donating of the price of a shot could make a man God on this street. The epaulets of this army of the lost wandering up and down in the sooty rain were the slumping defeated shoulders.

The Hollywood turned out to be a long room packed in between two other bars. Rude chalk lettering on the window advertised, "Wine, 15¢ glass." The number of bums inside was at a minimum, and I sensed from the look on the men at the bar, from the way they talked softly, hanging over their drinks like vultures, that they were professionals who used the street as a meeting place and clearinghouse. I moved to a deserted section of the bar and ordered beer. When the bartender brought it, I didn't drink.

"Seen Pat Tripp lately?" I asked.

The bartender, squat and harelipped, glanced down the dull wooden bar top. "No, I ain't seen him." His eyes registered fear as a slot machine registers the fruit.

"Where does he live?" I asked. "I want to see him. I'm a friend of his."

"I don't know that, either. I'm busy." He turned, but not so far that he could not see me pull out my wallet, and then pull out the ten. His head swiveled left, then right along the bar and his hand flattened itself on the bar. Sweat glistened in the lines of his skin. I folded the bill into a small square and slid it under his palm. The fingers of the hand closed slowly, like a sea flower. The bartender whispered an address on Halstead. I wasn't quite sure that I'd heard correctly, but the man was already walking away. I decided I shouldn't press the matter, so I fixed what I thought I'd heard in my mind and went toward the street, past the stooped backs of the men leaning over the bar.

The rooming house leaned precariously out over Halstead. A dirty yellow cat regarded me from chip eyes as I walked up the steps. A piece of paper tacked to the inside wall displayed a list of tenants scrawled in pencil. Tripp had a room on the third floor. I climbed the creaking stairs, past layers of cigar smell and old cooking smell, past the second floor sound of two girls giggling hysterically. Bare bulbs hung like eyes at the landings. On the third floor I walked to the rear of the corridor and knocked on Tripp's door.

His voice called out weakly, "Who is it?"

When I told him, he shouted hoarsely, "Get away, get away from here!" I tried the door. It yielded a little but did not open. I shoved harder, feeling sweat wet on my neck. The door bounced and a chair slid out from under the knob. I stepped into the room.

Fatsy Patsy Tripp lay on a cot, shirtless, supported on one elbow. His chest was covered with a hideous criss-cross of dirty blood-stained Bandaids, and I could see the unhealed burn-scars on his skin.

Tripp lay on a twisted gray sheet. The room contained an assortment of old furniture, and a coating of grime covered the dismal brown wallpaper. One window at the rear looked out upon the rickety back steps of another building, and to my left, just in front of Tripp's cot, two curtains of some thin cheap material hung in a narrow doorway. Through the six inches of space between them I could see cracked linoleum and an ancient gas range. Over Tripp's cot hung glossy pictures of point-breasted movie starlets, most of them sweatered, their hair perfectly done, their capped teeth gleaming in alluring smiles, the hint of passion on their glycerined lips. A litter of movie magazines and newspapers spread across the floor.

In the instant that I closed the door and uprighted the chair Tripp had placed under the knob, I felt sorry for the heavy man lying on the cot, with the flush of pain on his face. Old reddish flesh flabbed down over his beltless trousers. If Fatsy Patsy Tripp had ever seemed remotely ominous because he had connections with the underworld of Al Asperito and the seventh man, he no longer seemed so. A hoodlum, perhaps even a killer, but still a hopeless ugly man growing old, tasting the bitter gall of disillusion, lying alone and forgotten on a mean cot high over Halstead Street. No, not a single person could fear him now. The sick man, in the room with its reek of iodine and stale cigarettes, could only be called pitiful.

And Tripp was frightened. I could see it in his

large perplexed eyes. What had happened to his chest could not have been an accident.

I went into the kitchen while his eyes followed me and took a straight chair back to the cot. I sat down and offered him a cigarette. He accepted with a tremor in his meaty fingers. "What happened to you?" I asked.

"Mr. Diamond, you ought to get out of here."

"Did you know Asperito had been murdered, Pat?"

He drew the wet cigarette end from his lips and his pained eyes met mine. "Yeah, the landlady told me. She heard it up on Madison, one of the bars. Al was pretty well known around here, you know."

I nodded. He breathed heavily as he supported himself on his elbow. "Lie down," I said. "I can talk to you that way."

"What you got to talk to me about?" he said cagily, lowering himself on the cot. He closed his eyes and clamped his teeth together. A couple of the Bandaids wrinkled on his chest as he moved. He rolled his head to the side so that he could watch me. "You think I had something to do with Al getting killed?" I didn't answer for a moment because I felt sure now that he *did* know something. He desperately wanted to convince me otherwise, so much so that he'd brought up the matter himself.

"Asperito died a few minutes after I got to his house that night, Pat," I said evenly. "Somebody knew he was going to talk to me, so they killed him before he could say anything."

"That's how you figure it, eh?" Tripp wheezed.

"That's how I figure it," I returned tonelessly.

"You know who killed him?"

"No," I said. "But you do."

His mouth came open, and his eyes veiled over defensively, but not before I saw the flicker of terror in them. He was holding his cigarette up over his chest, and when I spoke his hand trembled. A bright dollop of ash fell on his chest and he wriggled with the sudden sharp bite of it. He swiveled his head toward the wall. "I don't know," he said helplessly.

"But the man that killed Asperito *knew* I was going to meet him, Pat. You arranged that meeting, didn't you? In my office at the paper. Between that time and the time I found Asperito shot, you told someone about the meeting. You told the killer, Pat. Didn't you?"

"No." His head swung toward me again and he tried to rise, getting his left shoulder under him. "*No!*" he repeated savagely.

I stared at him. "You're a liar, Pat. You sold out your boss. Didn't you?"

Tripp seemed to be waging some internal war, some dark battle between fear and the desire to wipe out the anguish of what he had done. "Okay," he blurted softly, not able to look me in the eye now, "I fingered Al. But I didn't have no choice, Mr. Diamond. I swear that's the truth."

"Who did you tell about the meeting?" I persisted.

"I swear I don't know," he said.

I got up, kicked the chair back and glared down at him. "What do you mean, you don't know? You say you told someone about the meeting Asperito had arranged, and yet you tell me you don't know who you told. Did you talk to him over the telephone?"

"No," Tripp said. "I talked to him right here in this room."

"You tell me about it," I said. I made it sound like an order.

Tripp carried the cigarette to his mouth again with fingers that quivered. "I—I came back here after I saw you, Mr. Diamond. I walked right in and somebody sapped me. I went out cold. When I woke up, I was tied in a chair. I think it was the chair you're sitting on right now. The guy, whoever it was, he took my coat and shirt off me and tied my arms behind my back."

"Then it *was* a man?" I said.

"I can't be sure. I . . . yeah, I guess so. No woman could have talked like that. It was a man. I didn't know the voice, though; I don't know many of the boys in town. I just worked for Al, did errands for him when he told me to." Memory of Al burned accusingly behind his eyes.

"Go on."

"The guy had a handkerchief across his face, tied in back. And his hat down low so I couldn't see his eyes. He had the window all covered up with a blanket, and it was pretty dark. I was scared, Mr. Diamond. He told me that he wanted to know if Al was going to do any squealing. I said I didn't know what he was talking about. He said squealing, talking to the cops or the papers. He had a mean voice, Mr. Diamond. Mean and hard. I tried to move but I couldn't; he'd tied me pretty well. I knew that Al was going to meet you, but I didn't tell him. He thought I was holding something back, so he took a box of matches out of his pocket; you know, the big ones with red heads. I saw he had gloves on then. He lit one of the matches and stuck it against me, here." He tapped the scarred area of his chest. "It hurt like hell. He kept doing it, and after a while it got so bad I couldn't stand it. I told him about the meeting." Tripp's eyes rested sadly on the bandage pattern below his chin. "The guy hit me again and when I woke up, I could hardly move. He'd untied me, but my chest was killing me." His voice rose in protest. "I haven't been able to move since then, Mr. Diamond. He hurt me too much. Honest to God, I wouldn't have said anything but I just couldn't take it. Nobody could."

I nodded slowly. "I see, Pat. I don't blame you."

"You don't?" His eyes drew down to pinpoints between his heavy lids. "Not even when Al got murdered because of it?"

The bitter pattern of white crosses stood out in the gathering darkness of the room. The scars appeared to be craters in the tortured surface of some wild moon. "Not even when Al got murdered because of it," I echoed. I took my cigarettes out and gave them to him. "It's all I've got, Pat. Thanks for telling me."

"I'd tell you who the guy was if I knew," Tripp proclaimed, closing an eager hand around the cigarettes. "I'd tell you okay. If he killed Al, he deserves to get it. He hurt me plenty."

I knew he told the truth. And I had nothing more to say to him. I said, "Take it easy, Pat," and walked out of the room. Tripp lay staring after me, the pack of cigarettes clutched to his chest like a magic talisman. I started down the stairs, realizing that I'd been stopped at this point, too. Even if Tocca knew about Tripp, he would learn nothing. The seventh man had covered his tracks skillfully and well. A healthy respect for him had been born within me, mingled with the anger I already felt. Respect for a mentality that could predict behavior on such certain grounds that safety would always be guaranteed.

I stood on the porch of the rooming house wishing I hadn't given away my last cigarette. The rain had stopped, but the heat remained. Even in the heat, I thought to myself, the seventh man's mind works precisely. From the behavior of the men at Dwight's home on the night of the meeting, he had been able to predict with certainty which one of them would be most likely to take steps to thwart his plan. Asperito, unwilling to share his gains with anyone. The seventh man had refused to take a chance on Asperito's *not* attempting to stand in the way, and he had covered the angles well. He had gotten to Fatsy Patsy Tripp and made him talk, with a narrow margin of safe time left, true, but what he had learned had carried out his predictions, and he had killed Asperito to close his mouth. What could Tocca do against such a man? Where to now? To nowhere. A grim, bitter joke, burning my mind like fire; a joke played upon me, upon Tocca.

Played upon Pat Tripp, too.

I looked upward at the scabrous brick face of the rooming house. Somewhere up there a man lay in pain, surrounded by photographs and a handful of bright slick-papered dreams. A criminal, yes; but not a criminal like the seventh man. Though I knew Tripp had been outside the law, I couldn't feel the anger toward him I felt toward the seventh man. Why? Because of those photographs? Because of the pitiful quality of the dream world he lived in? It was a problem Charlie Parnell might have been able to work out. I couldn't.

CHAPTER VIII

I walked the long blocks back to the Northwestern terminal, climbed in my car and drove slowly through the darkening heat of afternoon. I didn't want to go back to the paper and I didn't want to go home. I wound the car in and out of Loop traffic for twenty minutes or so, up a one-way street and down the next, my eyes fixed mechanically on the bumpers of the cars that slid in and out ahead of me. My clothes clung to me in moist uncomfortable folds. At last I recalled a pleasant little cocktail lounge on Chicago Avenue, off Michigan, and it gave me a goal. I drove north through the late afternoon maze of buses and yellow cabs, again working at the puzzle in my mind. I saw the fragmentary puzzle pieces disappear one by one, their edges squaring suddenly so that they would not fit.

First Rita Ray's face became distorted, then the piece belonging to Pat Tripp. That one had had a question mark printed on it once, a bright red question mark signifying hope, and now only a handkerchief-covered face stared out at me, topped by a hat, black and formless. The pieces fell apart like sand and my fingers wound wire-tight around the steering wheel as the pressure built up ounce by ounce within me.

A leviathan bus swung abruptly out in front of me with a sharp hiss of air brakes, and I caught a fragment of a driver's angry eye in the side mirror as I slid my Chevvy past the bus corner that projected like a boulder into a river. Almost an accident. Damn it, Diamond, I thought, you're losing your head. You're letting anger control you. If only the weather would change. If only the seventh man would make one wrong move. The *if* of Mr. Kipling would have my mind spinning in screwy, demented channels before long, I thought. When I parked, my hand shook as I released my grip on the wheel. I stared at the hand, the hairs curling on the back of it, as a country rubberneck watches a curiosity in the freak show.

The little cocktail lounge was air-conditioned and filled with vague purple light. I ordered one double King's Ransom and carried it into the cool comforting oblivion of a microscopic rear table. Once again I tried to rearrange the events of the past days into a sensible pattern. I produced a pattern well enough, but it ended abruptly in several places, and beyond those places lay the answer I needed and couldn't get. The fast lava flow of the Scotch down my throat blurred the edges of reality just enough so that I could light another cigarette from a fresh pack and notice that the tension tremor of my hand had vanished.

I decided to get in touch with Tocca again. The bug of anger had become a multicellular organism that grew with every moment, devouring and demanding more. No longer mere petty anger, either, but a consuming, almost hate emotion. The seventh man had covered his trail so well that with each discovery of a new part of the deception, my stubborn determination grew. I would take the gun from his hands and teach him to shoot at windshields.

Tocca gave me a short, cheerless greeting. "I wish you'd get off my neck, Diamond," he said through the crackling hollowness of the phone.

"I wondered how you were coming along on the matter of alibis."

"Still think it's your business, eh?"

"Yes," I said fast, "I do. I don't like being shot at and I don't like attempts to muzzle me, not by you, but especially not by a cheap hoodlum. I'm not trying to steal the thunder of the police department," I added.

"Okay, okay." The sigh whispered along the wire. "I suppose I've got to talk to somebody. Quinn can't help me, or he won't. Well, I've checked. Any one of the five men at Dwight's home could have killed Al Asperito. Any one of them could be the seventh man. The Ray girl stuck to her story, but we can't leave Bushnell out. They'll lie and cheat and do anything in the world to protect themselves, Diamond. I wish I knew where to go from here."

"Thanks," I said. The phone booth felt stuffy as a tomb. "Good luck, Captain."

A short tired laugh sounded over the wire. "Diamond, you're not a bad guy. Too nosey for your own good, but I guess it's an occupational disease. Even a guy in my line needs a little encouragement. I appreciate it." There was quiet sincerity in his words. After that we cut the conversation off and when I returned to the chilled purple atmosphere of the lounge, it no longer satisfied me. I decided to invite myself to Rosemary's for dinner. In spite of the mothering I knew I would receive, I needed a return to normalcy.

I drove up to Rosemary's place near Evanston and parked at the curb a few minutes after six. Rosemary, a damp lock of hair over her forehead and a plastic apron around her waist still looked remarkably cool and attractive in the peasant blouse and red ballerina skirt. She gave me a smile as I leaned wearily on the door frame. The smile could not be quite complete, however, since her eyes still showed worry and concern.

"Hi," I said. "Got room for an uninvited guest at the table tonight?"

"Of course, Harry. Come in." The apartment with its bright, modern colors and tasteful hominess came as a relief. Tow-headed Tommy gave me a quick greeting and then turned back to the squawking television set. I lowered myself into a comfortable position on a dark green hassock and Tommy and I entered into a scholarly discussion as to who was better, Captain Proton, or Space Ace, the latter currently on the screen, virile in his uniform, an all-powerful blasto-gun balled in one fist, a tight smile of sure confidence on his lips as he confronted the interstellar villains. It struck me that Tocca would be fortunate if he had a weapon such as a blasto-gun and a smile like that of Space Ace, supremely confident of the triumph of right. Those dreams, those illusions belonged only to the young, to Tommy and his companions in the third grade.

Rosemary served a crisp tasty meal of cold cuts and a salad. I drank nearly a quart of milk, and the talk ran mostly to what Tommy was learning in school.

Not once did Rosemary mention the Asperito affair, but consciousness of it showed in her lovely eyes every minute. I sat around and watched a couple of comedy shows on television, forced myself to laugh at the jokes, and left the apartment at nine-thirty. Rosemary took me to the door. I leaned against the door frame, making an effort at being casual.

"That was a fine dinner," I said. "You don't know how a guy like me appreciates a meal like that."

"I'm glad you liked it," Rosemary replied. We were fencing.

"Well, I guess . . ."

"Harry," she said. Her hand closed, cool on mine, and she bit her lip for a tiny space. "Harry, I've been doing my best all evening to—to keep . . ."

With my free hand I patted hers. "Look," I said gently, "don't worry about that any more. I've been working on my own temper, too."

"I hate myself for wanting to know, Harry, but—"

"Don't say that. What do you want to know?"

"How . . . how things are going?" Her eyes were averted, the "things" an obvious euphemism. The clean fragrance of her hair washed around me, erasing the old smell of summer heat.

I eased my hand from under hers. "Things are going fine. I'm taking good care of myself."

"For—forget I asked. Please."

I decided it was time to change the subject. "You've got a swell boy, Rosemary."

She glanced over her shoulder. Tommy was riveted in front of the television, and her smile was warm and full of love for her son. "He thinks you're pretty nice, too," she said, low-voiced.

"All kids have their daydreams," I said in a pseudo-flip tone. "They get over them."

"You can't be serious even if you try, can you?" she asked, smiling at me now.

"Very seldom," I replied. I waved myself away from the door as it closed behind me with a soft sound. I wanted nothing more than to have a boy like Tommy respect me and like me. But some vicious stubbornness balked inside me, fighting Rosemary when I knew I should not be fighting her.

The ride down to the paper was long and lonely, with the white headlights coming at me on the left and the red tail lights going away from me up ahead. The two streams of the world: The white of Rosemary and her boy; the red of violence and the seventh man.

When I arrived at the paper the fan was still whirling senselessly in the office. "Hi, boss," Artie said, getting up from the typewriter and stretching. His yawn sounded like a bull elephant's bellow. He handed me a couple of sheets of copy paper. "See what you think, will you?" He lit his pipe and leaned his elbows on the window, staring out into steamy neon-lighted night.

I read the copy. "It won't win a Pulitzer Prize, but it's pretty fair."

Artie turned, grinning. "Well, that sounds better than a slap on the belly with a dead whitefish, anyhow." He looked startled. "I forgot to tell you that Charlie Parnell called a little while ago. Said you should call him."

I rang up Charlie's desk. "You asked for information," Charlie said sourly. "I've got some. Word went out along West Madison this evening. Harry Diamond the newspaperman is looking for something."

"Does that have a special meaning?"

"The word doesn't pass unless it means something, Harry." His voice lowered. "I'd start being really careful. Your name's been chalked on the board of people to watch out for. They don't know what you're after, but they're curious, and when they get curious —well, they take more than a polite interest."

I thanked him. He grunted a monosyllable of gloom in reply and I hung up. Artie went back to work and I left the office. The night elevator man gave vent to his feelings on the weather and I nodded listlessly. My heels made a ghostly tapping in the dark lobby. I didn't want to go home, but I had no idea of what I *did* want to do. Michigan Avenue lay relatively deserted, only a few cars moving each way. The signals blinked red, yellow, green in colorful rows that stretched north. The restaurant across the boulevard showed lights, so I decided to get a hamburger and some more cold milk before I went home. Charlie's statement had set new wheels going in my brain.

I stopped on the curb to light a cigarette. No traffic was going by on my side of the street at the moment so I started across. Then to my left I heard the sudden sound of a motor whipping into life. I jerked my head around, already four steps out from the curb. The heavy black Caddy leaped out from the curb. Glowless headlights came at me like black monster eyes and the polished chrome bumper caught yellow slivers of light from the bright restaurant window across the way. I stepped back wildly and the

Caddy swerved, gaining speed, a black monster with opaque windows roaring down on me. My legs began to function then, scissoring frantically to get me back on the curb as the death engine roared closer with a harsh slicing of the air. In seconds I knew the seventh man was trying to kill me, and I fought to escape the juggernaut plunging over the concrete. My toe caught on the curb and I sprawled on the sidewalk, my cheek scraping against the rough surface. Brakes screamed. I got my knee under me and whirled like a trapped animal. A foot away the Caddy had stopped. Its engine purred softly.

I had my left leg twisted under me, my right leg bent, and I faced north in the position I had scrambled to after I first slid along the sidewalk. I had swung my head to the left so that I could stare at the black windows of the Caddy. I could see absolutely nothing through those windows, and a random thought chased across my mind: the syndicate even provided the seventh man with his own personal armored car. The scene lasted no longer than three or four seconds. I crouched, unable to move, as I heard the distant sound of motors on the boulevard, as I smelled the stale sweating air. The newspaper building sought the reddish night sky like a gigantic monument. My tombstone. In those few seconds I listened for the salvation sound of pedestrians coming along the concrete, but I heard none.

The moment I was coming erect my eyes focused on the right front window of the Caddy. The opaque glass which reflected light began to slide downward, revealing a widening line of black which reflected no

light at all: an eighth of an inch, a quarter, a half
three quarters, a full inch. Lightning fast it happene
then, I know, but it assumed the quality of a not
quite-real movie in slow motion.

Then I turned and dove headlong for the sanctu
ary of the revolving doors that led into the newspape
lobby. In the moment that I whirled to dodge, m
eyes had caught a glimpse of a tiny surface that re
flected light in the inky inch-wide line above the win
dow. A surface that jutted forward and became th
muzzle of a gun, round and gleaming as a small thi
doughnut.

Two steps from the building, even as I expected t
hear the sharp report that would mean a bullet in m
back, I heard another sound. I half-turned to th
right and saw that the traffic light beyond the rive
bridge to the south had turned green. A Yellow ca
cruised toward the newspaper, swinging around th
small curve so that its headlights picked out the glo
ing black sheen of the Cadillac body. Other hea
lights followed the cab, half a dozen pairs or mor
and the air on this side of Michigan filled with th
steady thrumming sound of engines. I stumble
against the stone building wall, breathing hard. Th
Caddy's motor raced and the Yellow cab swung ou
and around on the left side.

The inch-wide slit of darkness began to narro
and then it was gone.

The Cadillac's lights came on and it swung quickl
into the left-hand lane of traffic. A big Buick in th
right lane cut off the view I wanted of the plates.
followed the red tail lights of the Caddy for a bloc
or two, but my eyes blurred and I glanced away for

moment. When I looked again, the tail lights bobbed in a reddish sea, and it would have been impossible for me to tell one car from the other.

I staggered a step away from the building and clawed my necktie loose, shaking my head doggedly from side to side. I became aware of rapid, determined footsteps coming from the north. I saw a police patrolman angling in my direction, and without thinking I hurried away from him, down to the long steep stairway where I took the steps two at a time, stumbling once and feeling the hard angry pain bite up through my knee. I saw the patrolman looming like a giant in the ghostly light of an overhead bulb far at the top of the stairs and I started my downward flight again as he came down the first step. I practically tore my pocket out of my trousers getting my car keys loose while I ran. I never consciously thought about opening the car door and starting the motor. I only remember seeing the patrolman's face float by as he reached the bottom of the stairs and I pulled past. Savagely I forced the accelerator down and the Chevvy rocketed ahead. In the rear-view mirror I could see the cop fumbling inside his blouse for something on which to write my license number. The car spurted ahead again under my foot and I knew I had been too quick for him. The last thing in the world I wanted now was to talk to a cop.

The cigarette I lit tasted wonderful, and the hot stale wind fanning in through the windows was the most welcome wind that had ever blown in all the ages of time. As I drove north along the Outer Drive I congratulated myself on escaping; I reworked every detail of the situation, emphasizing in my mind how quick or how clever I had been. Above all, how damned lucky! I felt great.

After I had parked the car and gone into my apartment, the rage struck.

My hands trembled as I felt again the full impact of the death that had almost reached out to tap my shoulder. In the war I had fired a rifle on half a dozen sour, rotting islands of the South Pacific, but there had never been anything very personal in it. The enemy had been a great shapeless body of things inhuman, and I had had a similar fighting machine around me, of which I was a part. We didn't get into any hot corners, and it seemed like one machine versus the other. You felt no hatred that way. But the seventh man in the Cadillac—and I had no doubt that it had been anyone *but* the seventh man—had tried to kill me in all earnestness. The first target-pistol shot had been a warning. This was attempted murder, the sightless horror of dark headlights and the appearance of the thin-doughnut gun muzzle in the black bar of open window.

I fell onto the bed, my muscles rigid. Twenty minutes later I managed to undress, drink a beer and take a shower. The rage had not passed, only calmed until it was under control. Slow, low-burning hatred began to rise, reached a white-hot pitch even as it remained quiet. I threw no glasses at the wall and I broke no windows. But I moved calmly, methodically, rinsing the beer glass and replacing it on the shelf and snapping out the kitchen light. Naked and cooling I lay in bed. I could not be shaken now. Nothing in the world of God could keep me away from the chase. The seventh man had given the challenge, and as I lay there I thought of what I'd like to do to him. But the fate I preferred over all the others was to see him in the hands of the police. What would he really care if Harry Diamond shot him down? But the agony that would scream in his brain the instant before a police bullet spattered his life out, or a police cell clanked closed upon him! That would really hurt, because no man from the syndicate could hate a thing worse than the organized forces of law, nor suffer more than in their hands, with the knowledge of his own defeat.

I knew I could not predict the time or the place of the absolute end, but I knew what I wanted, and I wanted most of all to be the engineer who would have a hand in driving him to his final destruction.

I went to sleep finally with all the windows of the apartment open. When I awoke in the morning, rain had wet the sheets and chilled my skin. It blew in the windows now in gray, fitful gusts. I dressed quickly, feeling refreshed and mildly stimulated by what seemed the first good night's sleep I'd had in months.

As of now, I was through horsing around. Artie and Rosemary were perfectly capable of getting out the column. And I was definitely through playing the part of clay pigeon. From here on out, I was going on the hunt myself. I was as dedicated to my grim purpose of nailing that murderer as if he'd harmed or killed someone of my immediate family—and the fact that I didn't have any didn't change my feeling one little bit.

Through the drugstore window I saw Charlie Parnell, and joined him in the booth.

"I was going to call you, Harry," he said, after I'd ordered my coffee.

I leaned forward. "Something?"

He nodded as he rattled a spoon against the inner rim of the cup. "The town's waking up. The rats come out of the holes." His eyes probed at me from behind his glasses. "They had another meeting last night."

My coffee cup smacked loudly on the table as I set it down. "Dwight and the other four?"

"That's the information I picked up. They went across the state line, up into Wisconsin." His head wagged from side to side. "By God they're getting careful. But the tough ones in this town know that something is going to happen, and soon."

"What happened at the meeting? Do you know?"

"That's the kind of information that doesn't get passed around," he said. "But the mugs are putting the house in order. I wish I could stick a firecracker under that Quinn. Hell, I'd go into a monastery if I didn't like to watch the crooks wiggle. It may be Fourth of July before you know it, with unscheduled fireworks."

I excused myself hastily and left the drugstore. My mind worked rapidly now. Dwight had called his meeting to determine a city-side policy. Should they stand up to the seventh man or should they accept his terms? I had to know what had gone on at that meeting. I drove north along the Drive, five miles over the ten miles usually allowed on top of the legal speed limit. I swung around the Foster Avenue curve and headed north on Sheridan as the rain-bullets exploded in a steady stream on the windshield. If the town was stirring itself, then I was stirring with it. Devon went by, then Howard Street and the curve past the cemetery along the gray, storm-chopped lake. Up through Evanston, past the large homes set far back on spacious lawns, and the tires squealed around the long curve to the left past the dirty orange brick buildings of Northwestern. I braked at the corner and two sorority girls stepped out and around my bumper, glaring at me. I pulled on across the street and parked beside the Northwestern Union, heading for the phone in the grill downstairs, elbowing through a group of summer-session intellectuals blocking the doors. Back to college. The only thing I wanted from this college was a telephone, to lead me down the first road in the new campaign.

In the noisy chatter of the grill I wiped sweating palms on my coat. I could stop now, climb in my car and forget it. That would make Rosemary happy, I thought.

Then I thought of the Caddy that came out of the night, and I lifted the receiver.

CHAPTER IX

"Dwight Distilleries," announced the thin female voice on the other end of the wire.

"My name is Harper," I said carefully. "I wanted to see Mr. Dwight. Is he in his office now?"

I got channeled through to Dwight's personal secretary, and gave her the same words. She informed me coldly that Mr. Dwight would be in his office all day, but that I could not possibly see him until late afternoon, and only then by appointment. At that point I pressured the hook gently and the connection clicked dead. I went back to my car, congratulating myself on the way I was beginning to adapt to the rules of the new game. Light rain pestered the windshield when I eased the Chevvy up the long drive and under the portico. I smoothed out my suit as best I could and presented myself at the front door of the Dwight home.

Helen greeted me with a blank questioning stare that implied I should have used the peddler's entrance, the rear door.

"My name's Harry Diamond," I said a bit loudly. "I was here the other night, with Captain Tocca of the police. I'd like to see Mrs. Dwight, please. The word "police" brought a sharp expression of wariness into her eyes.

"I'll tell Mrs. Dwight that you're here." She ushered me into the huge front hall and hurried silently up the heavily carpeted stairs. The great chair stood ominously against the wall like the symbol of malevolent power, and unhealthy gray light seeped in from the dark day outside. I rolled my hat brim under my fingers for perhaps three minutes, and then Helen appeared silently, high at the top of the stairs. Without a sound she crooked a finger to beckon and I started up the long staircase. Helen did not move, and I noticed her severe mouth lift slightly at the corners, in an expression half envious, half mocking. When I reached the top she turned and led me silently down the corridor to an ornate white door. Helen opened the door, closing it again after I walked through.

The rug sank under my feet. I looked down a mile of carpet to where Linda Dwight rose from an embroidered love seat. She took off her gold-decorated shell-rimmed glasses and laid them on the book she had been reading, a collection of Kafka's short stories. Her gold lamé gown did justice to her slightly overripe, nearly matronish curves, or perhaps the gown only produced the heavier sensual effect of flesh. A stiff collar reached high and sweeping around the white neck and the fringe of black hair.

Behind the love seat, tall windows misted with gray rain opened on the somber view of lawn leading down to rocks, with the roiling lake whipping just beyond. There was a small bar in one corner, a large

Capehart radio-phonograph console, a metal type-writer stand on which stood a heavy Royal, and news-papers, magazines and sheafs of white typewriter paper strewn on the coffee table and the chairs. A half-opened door disclosed a large canopied bed. Linda Dwight certainly could not be put in the cate-gory of brainless women. She would be on her mental guard every moment, and the knowledge made me feel uncomfortable.

She advanced toward me, coral-tipped fingers at her sides, the gown belling out around her to show a pale area of ankle skin. The bodice was fastened pro-tectively all the way to the top.

"Should I be happy to see you, Mr. Diamond?" she asked with perfect politeness.

As I pushed aside some typewriter paper and sat down in one of her chairs, I had the feeling that I had suddenly become a stalked animal. She hovered be-fore me, demanding; the steady sheen of her eyes making it plain that I had to justify myself. I offered her a cigarette. She refused with a toss of her tight-curled black hair. Her hands remained steady at her sides, and she knew I was irritated by her calm.

"I doubt if you'll like what I've come here for, Mrs. Dwight." I lighted a cigarette.

"No, probably not." Mockery danced in her voice. "I don't like your column and I don't like you." Again she waited for me to continue.

I stood up, faced her squarely and her eyelids flickered a trifle, as if the move I made surprised her.

"Your husband went to a meeting last night, Mrs. Dwight, up in Wisconsin, with the same men who were in this house the night before Asperito died."

More surprise flooded her face now. "Did you go with your husband last night?"

"Aha!" She whirled around once and clapped her hands. The mockery in her gaze returned. "Harry Diamond is playing at detective. I wonder where you get your information."

"Did you go with your husband?" I repeated doggedly. The smoke from my cigarette lent a flat, stuffy feel to the air of the room. Rain whispered down the tall windows.

She inclined her head and said, "Yes. My husband owns a home in Wisconsin. The meeting was held there. Or had you heard that, too?" She studied me, trying to judge how much she should tell. As yet she had said nothing damaging, and she knew it. I got my next question ready when she said, "You want to know what happened at that meeting, don't you?"

"That's right."

She paced toward the windows, standing close to the panes, one palm pressed to the glass, her body slightly bent forward. "I know what went on," she said casually, her voice drifting back effortlessly from the direction of the glass. "I badgered Bill into telling me." She pirouetted toward me and I felt anger rise, because her lips wore a smile of complete triumph. "Very interesting," she admitted, and laughed. She walked toward me in slow, long-legged steps, each step as sure and as purposeful as the stalk of a tigress. "I have a price, Diamond," she said as she walked, the words emerging to blend with the fixed rhythm of her legs. "I'll trade my information for you." She reached me in a last swift step and her arms went around my neck, locking, and the greased slickness of her lipstick slid across my mouth. She pulled me downward against her, and I could see the black trace-lines of long eyelashes closed upon snowy skin.

I held her and kissed her, laughing inside myself because I knew I could win the game on her terms now. Self-centered as she was, she would be willing to sell the information for whatever pleasure she could get from something new. I said words that I thought appropriate and let her lock the door to the hall.

The information she gave as something worthless to her: Dwight and the other four had agreed unanimously not to enter into the proposed arrangement with the seventh man and his syndicate. Beyond that she knew nothing, or said she knew nothing, which amounted to one and the same thing. What Dwight's operating policy would be she refused to say. I thanked her, unlocked the door, and started to open it.

"You're good, Diamond," she said across the hollow room. "Poor Al, he was never very good at all." She spoke of Asperito as some kind of dead pet run over in the street and buried in the back yard. She was only too aware of the way her callousness disgusted me, but it didn't matter to her. "Come and see me again and we'll do some more trading," she said lightly. The door slammed shut. I let myself out into the hall, yawning, and made it to the car without meeting Helen.

The wipers ticked back and forth, slicing away the rain with the monotonous regularity of the heart beat of this rainy heated summer. I had learned what I wanted to know: Dwight and company refused to knuckle under. The seventh man would now have to try a new strategy, which meant a new threat to be waited for. What the threat would be, I couldn't predict.

And I had been initiated, really initiated into the game of chance and death. Linda Dwight had taught me the true meaning of deceit, the infinite heartlessness of the new world in which I traveled. Here, you had to fight tough. You had to fight dirty. I would fight that way, then. The rain mourned against the windshield as I drove.

The heat encamped over the city from gray bloated clouds pressing down on the concrete towers, arrayed from horizon to horizon like tents of a bivouacked army. I wandered thoughtless, useless and helpless from hour to hour while Artie Roth pecked out my column for me. Then I dropped in to see Tocca at headquarters. He immediately rushed me back out the door and into his car, explaining that he'd had enough of the imprisoning office. We found an air-conditioned restaurant on Monroe off Clark, a dark-walled restful place. Though it was still mid-morning, Tocca ordered three cheeseburgers and a large cold chocolate shake. He devoured the food greedily for a minute or two. A ragged stubble on his cheeks matched the black of his eyebrows. He needed help, and he couldn't get it by sucking noisily through a straw.

I explained about my visit to Pat Tripp, about the Cadillac that had smashed the night open and careened at me, freighted with death; about Linda Dwight and what had happened beyond the state line in Wisconsin. When I finished he gave a last rasping suck on the straw and set the glass on the table. I waited for him to raise his eyes and look at me. When he did, I saw no anger.

"You ought to get your ears beat down, Diamond," he said resignedly, "but I guess I just don't want to waste the effort in doing it any more."

"It's information," I said.

His jaw dipped in acknowledgment. "Right." He picked up the paper plate on which a cheeseburger had been served and began tearing it in small pieces. "You know, I'd enlist the damn Boy Scouts if I thought they could deliver the goods," he said with tight savagery. "I've got absolutely nothing. What you told me is nice to know, but it doesn't lead any place." His eyes riveted to mine. "You'd better watch your step, though. I won't step on you, but the seventh man will. He'll step, and hard!"

"He's already tried," I murmured. My stomach tightened as I imagined myself for a moment back on the sidewalk, the gun muzzle peering at me from the Cadillac window. I had an idea then, and I told him so.

His cigar traced pungent patterns in the clattering air of the restaurant. "Tell me the butler did it and I'm almost ready to believe you." The cigar stabbed toward me. "Every one of the five men sticks to his story. *Every* one. And *Quinn* doesn't think we need to go any further along that line! The snort he uttered was more heavy with disgust than an obscene word.

I spoke slowly, letting the idea take form as I went. "Captain, we grant that the seventh man is still in the city and still active. Do you think it would help any if

I started a series of stories in the paper on the crime in this town?"

Tocca frowned at me. "You mean exposé kind of stuff?"

I nodded. "If we laid it on thick, with pictures, the seventh man might decide that things were a little too tight at the moment and that he'd be better off to postpone moving in. That would give you more time to work."

Tocca's face wore the expression of a man who has awaited the punch line of a joke, heard it and convinced himself that the end of the story is not yet. I dug embarrassedly after a cigarette. "Is that your plan?" he said, but without mockery. I had to admit it was. Tocca's head immediately wagged from side to side. "Diamond, that's one hell of a poor strategy. Do you think the seventh man's going to be scared off because of some articles in a newspaper?"

"I thought anything would be worth trying."

"It's damned poor strategy," Tocca repeated.

Anger spurted up inside. "Hell," I exploded, "almost anything's poor strategy the way the seventh man's got you bottled up. What else can you do?" I gave him a moment, and his silence indicated that he could think of nothing. "Pour it on," I continued. "I guarantee I can make those articles the most sensational things that have hit Chicago in a long time. People will be shocked. But that'll help you. If they're aware of what's going on, for a day or a week or a month, you're better off than you are now. And if you can get some of the information O'Riordan was going to use pried loose from Quinn, the stories'll be that much better." I had leaned forward across the table without thinking, as eager to hammer my point home as any captain of a high-school debating team.

Tocca dumped the torn fragments of paper plate into his milk shake glass. His mouth pursed dubiously. "Maybe . . ." The one doubtful word lent encouragement. Though even I couldn't be thoroughly convinced of the worth of my idea, I forged ahead with a new angle that had occurred to me, feeling that effort of any kind had more value than no effort at all.

"Suppose the stories start the seventh man worrying," I postulated. "He might leave town for a while. But more likely, the New York syndicate would send one or two men in to help him back up his proposals if they saw it was too tough for him to do alone. You can get photographs of every known member of the syndicate, can't you? The FBI would help. Get your men to work memorizing those faces, and then I'll write the first story. Put your men at every railroad terminal and bus station, and at the airport. Watch for syndicate men coming into Chicago. They might lead you to the seventh man."

"Ninety chances out of a hundred it won't produce anything," Tocca said.

"But we've got ten chances out of a hundred that it might," I countered quickly. "Captain, it's a gamble. But gambling in this case is better than standing pat."

For a moment he remained silent. Tocca laced his hands around the milk shake glass and squeezed until the knuckles whitened. "I'll try it," he said to the table. "Provided I can get material for you from O'Riordan's file."

"We can play up one racket at a time," I said

eagerly. "We don't need to use the names of the men in charge, but we can hint at them. Captain. . . ."

His laugh came short and harsh. "You're making yourself a damned target. Why?"

The question threw me. At last I said, "He tried to kill me." He grunted and we talked on for a while, filling in details of the plan. Then, after a hasty handshake, Tocca left to see Quinn. If he failed there, I could forget about the entire operation.

At the office, Artie and Rosemary pumped me with questions I wouldn't answer. I wore a circular path on the floor in front of my desk. And when the phone finally rang, I jumped for it.

Tocca said, "I got it, Diamond. Quinn squalled, but I got it." The simple words hid a volume of conflict between this police captain and the man too small to sit in O'Riordan's chair. "I'll send a messenger over with it."

Tocca and I talked on the phone several more times that day. He wired Washington, and by nightfall photographs of every known member of the Eastern syndicate, from directors to one-job gunmen, were on their way to Chicago. By eleven in the evening three dozen plain-clothes men were at work at headquarters, poring over those photographs, memorizing scars and moles and peculiar twists of a nose, memorizing hairlines and ears that stood perpendicular to heads.

Rosemary and Artie had gone home long ago, Artie disappointed because I had taken him off several of the columns to come. The heartbeat of the paper roared on distantly down the long halls. Thunder crackled occasionally beyond the open window. I sat in shirt sleeves behind the desk, staring fixedly at the bulging manila envelope bound with rust-colored string on my blotter. My cigarettes burned away one after another. The heat bounced off the walls and pressed down on me. The phone rang, and I jumped, my slippery hand dropping the receiver onto the desk as I picked it up. Finally I had the receiver to my ear, the other hand tight on the chair arm.

"For the paper day after tomorrow," Tocca said. His voice sounded tired, but a new eagerness was there, too. "The men'll have the faces memorized by then. Start with Jake Bushnell and the dope racket." He paused. "Rip 'em, Diamond, will you?"

"I will," I said.

The night, the heat, the roaring silence of the building all vanished as I tore the rust-colored string loose from the bulging envelope.

CHAPTER X

I worked carefully, thinking out each word and organizing the whole into a coherent attack based upon the sheaf of papers that had been O'Riordan's chief weapon before the malignancy ate its way into his fighting heart. I used names and addresses: a pool parlor near Clark and Division, a soda fountain near one of the big north-side high schools; several more. Controlled anger beat down from my fingers as I drove the keys home, spelling out the whole rotten story of local dope-peddling for the readers, ending with a paragraph that listed the initials of the man in charge as J.B. I pulled the last sheet of copy paper from the roller and stared at it. I reread the rest of the material from the beginning, twenty-eight hundred loaded words, and felt compensated for the way my shirt wrapped itself around my chest in sticky folds. I locked the story, together with the retied file envelope in the bottom drawer of my desk, picked up my coat and snapped out the light. Through the open window I saw the S curve of the Outer Drive aflame with headlights. The Dad's Root Beer sign spelled out *Have You Had It Lately?* in neon. I laughed tonelessly and left the office.

Driving home, I had the feel of accomplishment.

Locked in my desk were twenty-eight hundred words, and now not only the city could be struck blindly, but the seventh man, as well. I slept soundly in spite of the heat. I had eaten breakfast and made my way to the photo morgue by quarter of nine next morning, though I only came up with one shot: a woman picked up in a raid on Sixty-third Street, her hand shielding her averted face, the needle punctures' black peppering shown clearly down the pale line of her arm on the gloss paper. The cheap print skirt was twisted up over bony knees as she sat trapped in the wooden chair, which I assumed belonged in a police station. With the print in my pocket I went to my office, unlocked the story and carried it to the managing editor.

It took an hour or two to clear it all the way to the top, and I was back in my office when the phone rang.

"Harry," the managing editor said, "they talked to Tocca from upstairs. The story is to go in tomorrow morning, page one lead, carried over to three. I'll send a man out to get pictures of the places you mentioned. One thing, though. That Captain Tocca suggested no by-line on the story. I called him, and he said he thought it was for your own good. What do you think?"

I settled deep into the chair, picturing the faceless seventh man. "I want a by-line," I said.

"Okay, suit yourself. You'll get the kicks, then. You can refer 'em to the legal department." A wry laugh echoed over the wire. "I guess we'll get some complaints, all right. You got something cooking with that cop, Harry?"

"Maybe." That terminated the conversation. Rosemary hadn't come in yet. I said to Artie, "You can go back to writing my column, wonder boy."

He grinned. "I'll get rid of you yet. But you know, you just restored my faith in human nature. I feel rejuvenated."

"You'll feel fired if you don't get to work."

"Yes, *sir!*" With a mocking salute, he went back to busily clacking the typewriter keys.

I left the office, glad that I could handle the complaints from the outset. Whoever countered the attack of the article might in some manner add another piece that would help the picture fit together. I had a cup of coffee in the drugstore downstairs, already nervous as I waited for eight o'clock when the first edition would slam down from the trucks onto the street corners and the people would read the story. I didn't care about the people. I wanted the seventh man to read my story as a personal letter.

The waiting tired me out. I arrived at the Lawrence El station thirty minutes ahead of time, and when the paper finally arrived I bought two copies, heading east along the dirty sidewalks, oblivious to the wet crowding humanity weaving in and out under the bar neons.

I locked myself in the apartment, stripped and sat before the fan, rereading each word. It was still good; the cuts had come out well, the needle punctures on the arm of the anonymous woman shockingly visible. In the morning came the first repercussion.

A Mr. Irving Prosser, counsel for Jake Bushnell was waiting in my office. Dressed in a faultless light blue summer suit, monogrammed white shirt and conservative print tie, he informed me that his client

Mr. Bushnell was considering legal action against the paper. Prosser stood ramrod stiff, left hand thrust deep into the patch pocket of his suit, right hand clasping a thin glistening-surfaced leather brief case against his hip. He awaited the effect of his pronouncement.

Seated behind the desk, I pressed the balls of my index fingers against a pencil and said, "Mr. Prosser, your client can take whatever action he likes. We have our own legal department to represent us. I think I ought to remind you, though, that no names connected with your client were mentioned in the article. Only the initials J.B. If you consult a phone book, you'll find a couple of hundred people with those initials. This sounds like an admission of guilt."

Prosser's smooth blue-cheeked face grew angry as he bent forward. "I don't play games, Mr. Diamond. Mr. Bushnell knows who you meant. I can also remind you that any idea you have of writing up this interview would result in more serious action." His black eyes showed hard, vicious surfaces.

"Non-legal?" I said softly.

"Yes," he replied crisply.

I released the pencil. It dropped softly on the blotter. I stared Prosser down. "The door's behind you, Mr. Prosser."

His mouth snapped open, then closed. He fastened a firm grip on the brief case, lifted his blue-banded Panama from a chair and walked out, mirror-polished black shoes clicking in determined rhythm as he vanished toward the elevators.

A week passed.

One additional complaint was registered by the

soda fountain, but the complaints stayed just complaints. Tocca became convinced of the fruitlessness of the plan, and consequently bitter toward himself and toward me. One week from the appearance of the first article came the second, on the clearinghouse for hoodlums run by Otto Schloss. The morning following the appearance of the story, I got off the elevator to be met by Rosemary and Artie.

"Harry," Rosemary said, stepping to the side of the hallway, "there's a man in your office, I think he's got a gun." Her hands folded restlessly over a fragrant bit of handkerchief.

"He's got a gun," Artie said in support. "So damned big you can see it hanging in his pocket. He's blowing his stack, spouting German right and left. . . ."

That meant Schloss. "Okay, thanks," I said, new twists of cold in my stomach. I patted Rosemary's arm. "You two stay out for a while."

I glanced to the information desk where Zabeck, burly and uniformed, sat on duty. Zabeck, I knew, had a heavy revolver in his desk drawer. "Tell Zabeck what's happening," I said briefly to Artie, "and both of you stand by." Feeling exhilarated, I started down the hall. I did not want to look more at Rosemary, and make her ashamed of her fear.

Otto Schloss wheeled like a maddened bull when I stepped into the office. I closed the door quickly and my eyes picked out the heavy pistol outline, badly concealed in the pocket of the sagging black coat. He still reminded me of an antique dealer, cheeks flushed a healthy red, drooping off-white mustache dotted with perspiration. I slowed my walk purposely as I circled him and sat down at the desk. "What can I do for you, Mr. Schloss?"

"*Mistblatt!*" he rasped, flinging a copy of the paper onto the desk. "*Gott hilft mir, aber . . .*" The words spilled one upon another in an angry guttural cascade.

"Speak English," I said.

He breathed deeply, the lines in his face growing hard so that the mask of the benign old man vanished. "Herr Diamond, you are responsible for the article in your newspaper. You mention me. You accuse me."

"Only initials were used," I said carefully.

"Initials! My initials! I don't like such publicity, I don't like such things about me written. Any more, Herr Diamond, I will make bad trouble for you!" He spat the last through clenched teeth.

I came up out of the chair knowing I had to meet him on his own grounds. "Get out of here," I snarled. "See the legal department if you want to make a formal complaint."

"Complain, *ach!*" His right hand dropped into the black coat pocket and my mind ceased thinking as I vaulted around the desk and smashed my fingers down on top of his, inside the pocket. I wrestled the gun, a long-barreled foreign revolver, from his rather weak grip, I managed to open the cylinder and shuck out the loads. I handed him the revolver and he swung at me with his right hand. I blocked it and shoved him hard against the wall. He took his revolver then and left, murder glinting in his old eyes.

Breathing hard, I dialed Zabeck's desk and told

him to send Artie and Rosemary in. I tossed the bullets on the blotter.

And I had just time to sweep them into my desk drawer as Rosemary came rushing into the office on hurried clicking heels. I wiped my forehead with a handkerchief as she gripped my arms above the elbows, fingers digging in savagely. She stood less than a foot in front of me, breasts trembling with panic under her frilly blouse. The fresh smell of her drifted around me like a healing cloud and her eyes plunged like searching arrows deep inside of me. "*Harry!*" she gasped, blue eyes blazing their longing, and abruptly the stiffness left her. I had to fold my arms around her waist to support her as she fell against me, warm woman flesh clinging to the length of my body. I patted her back clumsily, my face buried deep in the perfumed smoothness of her hair.

Suddenly she broke away, a flush rising in her cheeks. One hand brushed embarrassedly at her hair and words caught in her throat. "Harry, I'm sorry, I——" She whirled and hurried out of the office, face reddened, white hands clenched in an agony of embarrassment.

Artie stepped discreetly through the door, but he knew better than to make a joke. He closed the door quietly. "She's in love with you, Harry."

"So what?" I saw instantly I had hurt him in my attempt to cover up the tangle of my own emotions. I jabbed a cigarette into my mouth and leaned out the window for a while, breathing the smoke-tanged air. Within a few minutes Rosemary returned, composure regained, and I'd settled down enough to tell them what had gone on in the interview with Schloss. Thankfully I recalled that I'd swept the bullets into a desk drawer the moment before Rosemary arrived.

Rosemary sat down and crossed her legs primly to show me she had control. "Every time you get into a fight, Harry, you open yourself to trouble. It could be used against you."

"Someone could bump that Bushnell, or Schloss, and you could be in plenty trouble," Artie said solicitously.

I whirled on them, cigarette smoke hot through my fingers. "Why pick on me? Why am I suddenly going to get in so much hot water?"

"You're inviting it, Harry," Rosemary said, making every attempt to keep her attitude impersonal. "Kill or be killed. So you kill. The police could say that. Word of the fight will get around. It happened with Asperito."

"Borrowing trouble," I said, more to myself than to them. I sat down sourly at the desk, the half-inch of butt beginning to scorch my fingers. I'd made an enemy, certainly. But Rosemary had worked herself up over the fact that I could have easily been a suspect in the Asperito business. I shrugged off the thought as foolish.

I phoned Tocca immediately after that and told him what had happened. He replied with a noncommittal monosyllable, then hesitated. I could hear his breath rasping across the connection. I kept silent, waiting for the words I knew would come.

"Roblein left town last night," Tocca said harshly.

"*What?*"

"That's right, he took a plane out early in the evening. Checked through to Dallas. We lost him there, but I put some tracers out, figuring he might try for Mexico. And he did. He's on his way to Acapulco. Like that?"

"No," I said.

"I'm going to check Roblein's downtown office. Want to come along?" I said I did. "Meet me on the south-east corner of State and Jackson, half an hour." His breath ripped over the phone explosively. "Diamond, the thing's rolling."

Tocca stood on the appointed corner, close to the building, a shiny green slicker wrapped around him against the drizzle. He saw me and immediately turned east along Jackson as I fell into step beside him, striding, like a machine. At Wabash, we stopped under the shadows of the El and a train racketed by overhead, filling the shadowy streets with ominous thunder. On half a block through the drizzle as I kept silent, forcing down the thoughts that plunged like stallions under the first bit. I wouldn't let them free, not until I saw for certain what this change of events meant.

The elevator slid us up noiselessly to the eighth floor of the office building. Tocca went ahead of me again, eyes flicking along the ancient brown wooden doors until they lit on the ground glass panel whose stenciled lettering read, *Roy Roblein Enterprises*. Tocca opened the door and we entered a one-room office containing a scarred desk, a chair behind it, a large gray enameled filing cabinet in one corner and a dozen telephones arrayed on top of the desk. It required only a little imagination to visualize this grimy-walled office as the center of Roblein's web of women.

The lanky black-rooted blonde uncrossed her legs and stood up, pulling the cigarette away from the glue of her precisely penciled lips. She wore a wine skirt and a mannishly tailored gray vest over a white blouse, but the vest swept low enough to give a fine idea of her cleavage. The confession magazine she put down brought confidence into Tocca's eyes. He slammed the door sharply.

"Yes?" the girl said with formality. Her face had a blotched appearance beneath the semi-orange pancake. She gave an imitation of a Boston sneer.

Tocca showed her his credentials and the sneer collapsed. "Roy Roblein left town yesterday, correct?"

"That's right, Officer," the girl stammered. She searched the walls helplessly for assistance, found none. Nor on the cover of the confession magazine.

"Who's in charge?" Tocca snapped.

"In charge?" The girl gaped blankly. "I'm in charge of the office. In charge of what?"

"Roy Roblein Enterprises," Tocca said with contempt, lifting his thumb over his shoulder at the lettering on the door. One of the dozen phones shrilled and the girl stared at it in terror. Her hand reached for it automatically, then the fingers folded inward, nails biting deeply into her palm. She watched the phone with such heaving breath that you could almost hear her words of prayer that it would stop ringing. At last the jangling noise died away. Sweat formed a delicate mustache on the girl's upper lip.

"I'm—I don't know who's in charge, sir," the girl said. She spoke the words with her eyes averted.

Tocca stepped forward, jaw jutting and pointed accusingly at the metal filing cabinet, another object the girl suddenly wished would disappear. "Listen," Tocca said with quiet ferocity, "I'm not on the vice squad, but if you lie to me I'll rip that thing open and take out the names of a few of your high-priced queens. That'll be enough to put you away for a dozen years or so. Understand?"

Even though Tocca was obviously bluffing her, she took him literally, and collapsed into the chair, her face breaking up as if her features had individually come unglued. "I don't know who's in charge, honestly. Someone from out of town. A man called me up this morning when I came to work and said he was taking over for Roy—Mr. Roblein. He didn't give his name. He only said I should stay here on the job. That's all." Tocca advanced toward the filing cabinet around the desk corner. The girl's fists whirled in helpless little circles at her hips. *"That's all!"* she shrieked softly, and the fitful sobs covered the end of her last word.

Tocca glanced at me, and nodded. That *was* all she knew.

Tocca took her name and address, verified it from the wallet in her handbag and warned her to be careful. She understood the full implication. Her shoulders heaved faster, the sobs came more wildly, and I was glad to leave the office.

"The seventh man's in," Tocca said as we walked along the rainy street. "Our pretty little plan fouled itself up. Diamond, we couldn't watch every high-way, could we?" I said nothing. "The syndicate sent a guy in to take over, or maybe it's the seventh man himself. Anyway, he got to Roblein and bought him off." Tocca's eyes swung to mine, the curtain of rain falling shroud-soft between. "He's *in*, Diamond," Tocca said with suppressed violence. "He's in the town and he's breaking things apart so he can pick them up his way." Tocca gazed helplessly at the sky. "My God!" he whispered.

We caught a cab, and I rode with him back to headquarters because he said he might have some-thing new on Roblein. Two minutes after we'd arrived in his office, a sergeant entered and handed Tocca a yellow teletype sheet. He scanned it, then asked the sergeant: "When did this come in?"

"Twenty minutes ago, sir." Tocca dismissed him and handed me the paper, face completely bleak and lifeless.

According to the message, Roy Roblein, American citizen, had been run down and killed as he was leav-ing the Acapulco airport. The local officials regretted that there seemed to be no trace of the car that killed him. The words blurred. Big Roy, dying in the sun during the first moments of his vacation, chrome fire from a car bumper smashing his eyes, wheels across his head. The seventh man made his arrangements with permanence in mind . . .

Tocca asked me to leave. He wanted to think. As I closed the door I heard him ripping paper, and he whispered curses.

CHAPTER XI

Tocca's next move was obvious, except for the fact that it would be virtually impossible for him to accomplish it. He had to prevent the seventh man from making further contact with the other political and underworld leaders of the city, prevent him from eventually gaining complete control of Dwight's proposed organization. But he was balked by the fact that no matter how much he wanted to do just that, he had no authority. His only hope lay in unmasking the seventh man for the murderer he was, and from my corner it appeared that Tocca stood no closer to that now than he had been on the first night, when we sat in Asperito's living room. Even if Tocca had possessed the power to prevent the seventh man from making further contacts, I saw no way he possibly could have done it.

Heated rain slammed my windshield with renewed savagery and the towers of the city dissolved against the sky. In my imagination, a giant clock inched out the minutes and the hours until the time came when nothing remained but passive resistance.

The quiet halls of the newspaper near ten in the evening seemed a safe and remote haven. In my office, I stripped off my sodden coat and threw it on a chair as I lit a cigarette. The cubbyhole remained still. I got busy reading over a sheaf of notes Artie had made for the column, and several minutes later, my eyes still on the heavy handwriting, I listened, knowing someone had come down the hall.

Linda Dwight stepped out of the shadows into the office, cool and remote in a mint-green traveling suit. A mottled cream-colored Samsonite suitcase rested beside her high-heeled feet. I rose, glad to see even her. Words came as a release from thinking. Her eyes for once showed concern in the harsh unbeautiful glare from the ceiling.

"Come in," I said.

"Thank you." She refused my offer of a chair but came forward to the desk, leaving the bag in the doorway. She turned down a cigarette, too, and it pleased me to see the worry in her dark eyes. "Mr. Diamond, I—I came to ask a favor." Her tone implied that she knew I stood in a good position to turn her down flat. The silent testimony of the suitcase puzzled me, though.

"The heat affects my virility," I said with veiled sarcasm. "I'm afraid I wouldn't be much good tonight. Besides, I don't need any information. My trading days are over."

Her eyelids flickered swiftly. I knew she wanted to spit derision at me, and I enjoyed her helplessness. "Mr. Diamond," she said softly, "is it true that Roy Roblein was murdered?"

That startled me. A moment afterward I replied, "According to the police."

She examined her dark green cotton gloves. "Well,

thank you. That's what I wanted to know." She gave the right glove a tug, smoothing it back over her wrist. Her shoulders lifted slightly, as if they had been driven up by stiffening determination. "Bill mentioned it to me this evening. He's rather disturbed. I thought that if it was true, it was time for me to pack up and leave. Bill wasn't sure, you see . . ."

I laughed.

"What's funny?" Anger flickered like black lightning in her eyes.

"Nothing. I only thought you were perfectly at home in your husband's world. It shows how wrong you can be, doesn't it, Mrs. Dwight?"

"I'm perfectly at home anywhere," she returned with a chill smile. "But Bill's in really dangerous territory, Mr. Diamond. I can do better for myself somewhere else, that's all."

I studied her. "Do you ever get tired of business deals?"

"Sometimes, yes," she admitted, with surprising quickness. "When I was in high school, Mr. Diamond, I went to the senior prom with a boy." Her voice echoed, her eyes mirrored the lost corridors of time. "A typical prom night it was, a full moon and a soft wind and all the girls in beautiful dresses. I didn't know any better." Her eyes snapped back to me. "The boy made me pregnant and I went into a charity hospital after my parents turned me out. That taught me something. Only when I'm foolish do I remember that night and how it was, the warm wind, the moon that was hackneyed because it was so real. I *felt* that night, Mr. Diamond. I lived one way, for one moment, but the consequences were too much. I decided after the child came that emotions always cost too much." Her lips fixed in a tiny blank smile.

"I'm sorry for you," I said.

The smile remained fixed. "That's not necessary. There are more men like Bill; many more. I'll get along very well. Good-by." She turned quickly, caught up the bag and her heel-taps faded down the hall to the elevator. Yes, I felt sorry for her now, not disgusted or angry any longer. She'd made a bad trade at the very start. The coldness in exchange for giving up the hackneyed moon. Well, I suppose she couldn't help herself. . . . She'd travel only via air, of course, and be sipping Martinis in New York tomorrow.

I left the building where my friends worked earnestly on the paper and drove slowly home. I mixed gin and orange juice and sat in the kitchen with the cold chrome of the table edge pressing against my naked belly.

The phone jangled in the dark front room. I put down my drink and padded toward it on bare feet.

I stumbled against the phone table and got the receiver into my hand. Street lights traced eerie witch patterns on the ceiling as their light filtered through the window. I wondered who in hell would be calling me.

"Hello," I said.

"Herr Diamond?" The voice came in a hush, and surprise blasted all the way down to the soles of my feet. Schloss!

"Speaking." My tongue caught in my mouth, thick with astonishment.

"*Schloss, ich bin . . .*" He spoke breathlessly.

"Wait a minute, Mr. Schloss. I can't understand German."

"I'm sorry," he mumbled. "It is just that I am so excited." He left the remark in the air. I waited, heard nothing more and asked him what he wanted.

"Please, I must ask for your help, Herr Diamond. I am in trouble and I beg you to help me. I have information which I think you would value."

Every nerve in me came alive. I knew what this might mean, but I deliberately forced my hopes back down. "You want to make some kind of an arrangement?" I asked. "A deal?"

"*Ja, ich*—forgive me, yes, Mr. Diamond. A deal. That is it."

For the first time I had been given a break. My fingers choked around the handle of the phone as if I was afraid it would suddenly disintegrate before I could hear him out. "Go ahead. I'm listening."

"As I said, Herr Diamond," Schloss went on in his soft, urgent gutturals, "I have information concerning the activities of the Eastern syndicate." He gave deliberate emphasis to the last two words. "You are sure to be interested." He sounded as if his life depended upon my being interested.

"If you've got something worthwhile, Mr. Schloss, we'll make a deal." I fumbled for a cigarette and held the receiver with my chin while I lit it. I dragged deeply. "When can we talk?"

"Now," Schloss insisted. "It must be right now."

"Why are you coming to me, Mr. Schloss? I thought you wanted to kill me."

"*Bitte*—please," Schloss replied explosively, "my animosity I must forget. I am in trouble and you are the only person I know who can help me. I forgot what I have done because you would benefit by helping me. *Do you understand?*" he finished desperately.

A car horn blatted loudly out on the street. "What kind of trouble are you in?" I asked.

His voice lowered until it was barely audible. "The representative of the Eastern syndicate who placed the note on the table at Herr Dwight's has contacted me."

"In person?"

"*Ja.*"

"You know who he is?"

"*Ja.*"

So Schloss's bargaining power came from knowing the identity of the seventh man. He wouldn't be stupid enough to tell me over the phone. "Go on," I prompted.

"This person who contacted me offered me a sum of money for vacating my position at the head of my business. He also offered me immediate airplane space to South America. I accepted his offer. I had no choice. He gave me the airplane ticket, but I do not receive the money until I arrive in South America. I am no fool," Schloss spat quietly. "I know what happened to Roblein in Mexico. When I reached South America I would be killed. I want to leave the city tonight. I can go to Europe. They will not find me there. But the person representing the syndicate has *already* taken over my business. You understand me, Herr Diamond?" I said I did, all too clearly. "I cannot touch my personal finances now. The airplane for South America departs at ten tomorrow morning. I must be out of the city by then!"

"Where are you now?" I asked.

"I am in a phone booth near my apartment. I left my apartment a few minutes after the syndicate person departed. He was with me less than an hour ago. I packed a few clothes . . ."

"The police would protect you," I said.

He cursed bitterly in German for a moment. "Police! Then I would remain in this city and I would be a *dead man!*" The ends of his sentences received short emphatic punctuations of breath. "I will sell you the name of the person from the syndicate, Herr Diamond."

"For how much?"

"One thousand dollars in cash. The price of a one-way flight across the Atlantic."

I twisted one nervous hand through my hair. "Damn it, Schloss," I said desperately, "I can't raise that kind of money tonight. Not until the banks open in the morning."

"Then I shall have to try elsewhere." His voice fell, and for a moment I was afraid he would hang up. Then I realized that I was probably his *only* hope, and that he wanted me to think of something that would enable us to do business. God knows I wanted the name of the seventh man. Yes, I was right. Then the sound of his irregular deep-chested breathing whispered over the phone wire.

"A trusted friend has agreed to drive me from the city at five o'clock tomorrow morning," Schloss said tentatively. Five o'clock. That was my deadline. I reasoned that if this one solitary friend has sufficient money, Schloss wouldn't bother phoning me. My mind fought the deadening heat and came up with a possible answer.

"We can work it, Mr. Schloss. You leave at five o'clock and I'll wire you the money. To a bank in whatever city east of here you want, say by eleven o'clock, Chicago time, tomorrow. Cleveland? Buffalo?

"That means I must trust you and give you the name before I leave."

"That's the only way we can do business."

Schloss sighed tiredly. "Very well. You will promise not to release the information to the police until twenty-four hours after you make payment to the bank." I said I'd agree to that. I'd almost agree to putting on a Foreign Legion uniform for life to know the name that Schloss had locked in his tormented, fear-ridden brain. I glanced at my watch. A few minutes before twelve.

"Look, Mr. Schloss," I said urgently, "you'll need a place to stay until tomorrow morning. Your apartment isn't safe. Come here." I gave him my address and he repeated it. That quick response to my suggestion showed me how desperate he was. "Phone your driver and give him the address, too. We can sit up all night." The man who had only today wanted to kill me, I now offered to protect. Strange how the world suddenly altered its pattern in a few short hours.

"Very well," Schloss whispered. "I will come soon."

A new thought struck me and I told him to wait in the vestibule if I wasn't there when he rang. He grew frightened but I told him that I had something important to do, for his own protection. And mine, I added silently as I hung up.

I stood for a moment in the sticky darkness, wondering how I had managed to come through the interview without botching it. At a dozen different places I could have said the wrong thing and frightened him off permanently. Luck. Perhaps before the night broke I'd have the answer. Luck that brought the hateful determination.

I dressed rapidly, stuffed cigarettes into my shirt pocket and picked up my car keys and wallet. Then I let myself out of the apartment and climbed into my Chevvy at the curb. I twisted the wheel and the Chevvy spurted out of the parking slot, the right fender shaving clear of the rear of the car ahead by a fraction of an inch. Luck again. Desperate luck, and I was rolling sevens one after the other. I had to keep rolling them all the way down the dark alley of the night until I came out a winner in the dawn, with a name.

Along the Drive, I kept the accelerator to the floor, listening to the smooth roaring precision of the motor as I speeded south. I cut down North Avenue to LaSalle and made my way to the top floor of a run-down dirt-grimed apartment building, and knocked on a door. A moment later Charlie Parnell stood framed in a square of light, cigarette smoke clouding behind him. Charlie was wrapped in a bulky red corduroy bathrobe, and without his glasses his face appeared to sag. Behind him I saw an easy chair in a cone of light from a cheap bridge lamp, and piles of books retreating into the shadows.

"Harry!" Charlie grinned, but with puzzlement in his feeble eyes. "Come on in."

"Charlie, don't ask any questions. Have you got a gun I can have for the night?"

"Sure, Harry." He bent his head forward as if trying to understand, then blinked. "Wait a minute," he said, and disappeared beyond the lighted area. In a couple of minutes I heard Charlie's slippers approaching, and he held out a short-barreled revolver. "I've got this, Harry. It's a thirty-eight." He handed it to me.

"Thanks," I said, glancing at the brutal snubs of the loads in the cylinder. Charlie reached out a thin finger. He showed me that the safety was on. I slipped the gun into my pocket and felt its weight there.

"You in trouble, Harry?" he asked.

I hit him on the shoulder, and laughed. "No, Charlie. I've got luck tonight. I'll explain later. Believe me, it's worth waiting for." I turned to go, mentally counting each wasted second.

"Watch out for that gun," Charlie warned. "I haven't got a permit for it."

"I will, Charlie. Thanks." I was already down the black hole of the stair well. Along the line of the floor I caught a last glimpse of Charlie framed in the door, childish and sad in the bathrobe that had been made for someone else. . . .

In my car again, I made a wide tire-screaming U turn on LaSalle and started north hitting every green light on the way to the Outer Drive, where I started weaving in and out of lanes, making time. I laughed when I thought of the way I'd hit the lights just right. Keep it up, my mind said. Keep it up, and you'll get him. *Don't let the pattern break . . . !*

CHAPTER XII

I finally found a parking slot between my apartment and Sheridan Road. I got out of the car and started along the dark sidewalk, losing some of the confidence I had previously had in the ordered pattern of things. My feet drummed loudly on the pavement. I glanced behind me and saw a car door open and a shadow of a man emerge onto the sidewalk, silhouetted against the neons on Sheridan. He lit a cigarette, puffed it to life slowly and threw the match away in a lazy spiral. I walked faster. The street possessed an ominous sense of waiting. I searched the sidewalk ahead. An oblong of yellowish light fell onto the sidewalk from the vestibule of my building. I turned again, slowly and carefully, and saw the man who had lit a cigarette strolling behind me, hands in his pockets.

A shape materialized from under a dark tree and a hand closed on my arm. "Herr Diamond," came the panicked whisper. "I could not wait in the vestibule. It was too light."

I slid into the shadows, catching the heavy smell of Schloss' old-fashioned clothing. I slipped my hand into my jacket pocket, fumbled for the safety on the

.38 and threw it off. The revolver felt cold and slippery in my palm.

"Were you followed?" I whispered to Schloss. The man with the cigarette had stopped to peer questioningly at the sixth building away.

"*Nein,* I do not think so. I took a taxicab from the drugstore where I phoned you to the El. I caught the train as it pulled out. No one got on after I did. I am sure, Herr Diamond."

My nerves hummed. I wasn't so sure Schloss hadn't been followed. I took his elbow. "Come on. We'll go out to the alley and in through the basement, just in case."

I heard footsteps clacking through the humid air behind me. "In here," I whispered to Schloss, guiding him into the long black areaway. As I turned I saw the man with the cigarette coming at a fast walk. I started forward through the sweaty brick tunnel along the side of the building. Schloss stumbled once, cursed thickly in German and I pushed him on. We reached the alley, a long black corridor running along the garages behind apartments facing Lakeside and Leland Avenue. I urged Schloss to the left, taking one final look back up the areaway. The man with the cigarette stood stolidly before it on the sidewalk, his shadow-body filling the rectangular entrance. After another step I collided with the iron railing of the stairs leading to the basement door. Schloss went ahead of me and I heard the protesting squeak of the handle.

I was almost inside when a car's headlights blazed to life in the alley. I slammed the door behind me as I heard the motor start. Schloss whirled, lips pressed

together, his eyes rounding with fright. His hat had
fallen off and the nimbus of white hair seemed to
writhe, Medusa-like. My hand slid along the wall
and flicked the switch. Down a path between stacked
barrels and crates a light snapped on under a green
tin reflector. The gray service elevator door glinted
dully. Schloss started forward again as the motor
roared for an instant in the alley. The car stopped
again outside the door, I heard a slam, and feet
slapped down the cement steps.

"Ach, Gott, wir sind . . ." Schloss moaned, his
head rolling. We stood by the service elevator now.
I thumbed the button desperately and hope slipped
away in the instant I saw the red glass eye blink on
with the black letters, *In Use.* I drove my hand into
my pocket and felt the gun tangle in the fabric lining.
Schloss wailed in soft Teutonic syllables. The basement door banged open as my fingers twisted the gun,
struggling to get it free.

Another man was coming inside, a slanted Panama
brim across his forehead. He held his gun before him
and the gun snarled and spat, echoes coughing down
the row of barrels. Schloss gave a little cry and fell
back against the elevator door, his mouth open, one
hand knotted into the fabric of his old-fashioned
black vest. I slid on my face along the pebbly concrete,
lining up the revolver and hoping my nervous system
would pump me full of enough adrenalin to make me
remember what the war had taught. It seemed like
eons while I executed the slow trigger squeeze the
Negro sergeant had drilled into me. The Panama hat
tilted as stud eyes swept along the floor to line me up.
The barrel of his gun shifted toward my head.

Squeeze. . . . The revolver coughed, and the other man's gun clattered to the cement floor. He rose to his full height, whirled around, and then fell out the door, sprawling across the steps, his Panama rolling several inches.

I lay there, waiting. I could see the headlights still glowing, but the car doors remained closed. There were only two of them, then. I got my feet under me and scrambled up. Schloss had slid all the way down to the floor, and small sounds came out of his mouth. Abruptly the door slid backward, opening, and light poured out of the emptiness. What could I use an elevator for now?

I knelt by Schloss and unbuttoned his black vest. The spotless starched white shirt displayed a ragged bright red splotch that widened even as I watched it. Schloss rolled onto his side, fists pressed to his temples, scrubbing his hips along the concrete as if he could wipe out the pain. I didn't open his shirt. The shot had opened his stomach.

Schloss' left hand shot out and closed on my belt, constricting there. I bent closer to him, feeling the sweat run down my nose. The elevator door clanged closed suddenly, and the elevator began to whine upward, the sound retreating into the high distances of the building. Schloss twisted my belt and rolled from side to side.

"Gott! Gott! Gott . . ." The words fell from his lips in measured beats of pain.

"Schloss, can you hear me?" I whispered. "Can you understand me?"

He gasped for air. *"Verstehe . . . ja. . . . ich versteh. . . . Gott!"* His eyes snapped open. "Diamond, *ich*—I die!" he said in the small monstrous voice of desperation.

"Schloss," I said, "you've got to listen to me. Who came to see you tonight? Who was the man who came to see you? *Schloss!*" The words came out in a soft harassed shout. *"Who came to see you?"*

"I hurt so, Diamond. *Bitte.* Please. Can . . . you get me a doctor now?"

The elevator sound came closer again, whining downward. "I tell you . . . *Lieber Gott!*" The red splotch had widened all the way across his stomach now. He doubled up his knees and whimpered in German. Words came out of his mouth in bubbles of saliva. I shook his shoulder harder than I should have.

"In English!" I said. "Who was it?"

His eyes focused on mine again, metal-bright from the bulb over the elevator door. His hand held fast to my belt. "Diamond . . . *ja* . . . I tell—he came . . . *ja* . . . fear, Diamond. Fear, fear . . . he came . . ."

"Who *was* it?" I shouted. The elevator roared down from the first floor with the sound of a thundering dynamo.

Schloss got his elbow under him and he raised up. The other hand twisted my belt harder. His eyes sought the tin-shaded bulb as if it were the sun and his face hardened into fanatical frenzied lines. *"Fear! Fear!"* He cried the words to the electric sun and then fell back exhausted. His lids flickered and the words trickled off in a dry whisper. His eyes closed completely. His head moved, falling to the side a fraction of an inch. He stopped breathing.

I knelt there like a blind man, bitter gall of defeat stinging me. I felt the gun in my hand and looked at it stupidly. And suddenly the elevator door opened with a metallic clang that came like the sound of a world ending.

My head whipped up. From the distorted angle I saw the janitor, Paulson, standing tall like an avenging angel. His eyes widened as he saw Schloss, the gun in my hand. "Mr. Diamond! I heard shooting!"

I leaped up. My trousers tore at the belt as Schloss' dead claw hand ripped loose. The accusing eyes of the janitor scorched me. I turned and ran for the door.

I jumped over the body of the man I had shot and stumbled up the steps into the alley. A thin hot drizzle fell from the smudgy red sky. A glance into the areaway showed the bulk of the other man down at the far end, a lumped shadow against the backdrop of misty gold rain. Without thinking I ran west along the alley, my heels slapping wet concrete as I plunged along between the rows of garages. Suddenly I became aware of the gun still clutched in my hand. I plunged my fist deep into my pocket and left the gun there.

I started off at a walk, still heading toward Sheridan. At last I figured I was approximately opposite my car and I cut through another deserted areaway to the street. A moment later, I was sitting safely behind the Chevvy's wheel. The motor coughed alive with a roar that seemed to fill the world and rock the sky.

I drove north, again hitting almost all the lights on green, but now the luck I'd hoped for seemed only a black joke. I knew where I had to go. Something instinctive, deeper than thought, made me seek protection near Howard Street, when I knew there was no other protection in the city. I finally turned up at the door at Rosemary's flat, my car parked in the shadows on a side street two blocks away.

It took a couple of minutes for Rosemary to answer my ring. She brushed self-consciously at her hair the minute she saw me. The first thing she thought of were the bobby pins holding her hair tight to her head, and the scrubbed, no-lipstick appearance of her face. She looked beautiful. She looked at my clothes, and then my face.

"Harry! Are you in trouble?"

"Yes. Please, Rosemary, let me in." I was already through the door. She asked me a question I didn't hear while I rammed the door closed again and twisted the safety lock. Then I took a deep breath.

"Sorry I made so much noise. Tommy's asleep, huh?"

She nodded, her lips tight. We padded through darkness to the small kitchen, where she shut the door and plugged in the percolator. The rain tapped on the window that looked out on a deserted back porch. Finally I got a cigarette going. The percolator began to bubble with ghostly laughter.

Rosemary sat down opposite me, bundled in an old blue cotton bathrobe. Her hand slid across to close on mine. Her fingers were cool. "Harry, let me help you. Please tell me what's wrong."

"Listen," I said intently, trying as hard as I ever tried to make her understand, "I won't get you mixed up in this, Rosemary. There's nothing you can do for me, so for God's sake don't ask. Please." She studied me a   moment, then lowered her eyes and nodded only the tiniest bit. "Thanks," I said, amazed at the harsh sound of my own voice. "Rosemary, you don't know what's happened, and I don't want you to know. Just let me sit here and drink coffee, that's all I need."

I needed one hell of a lot more than coffee right then, I needed a miracle. But where could you find one in the bleak rainy hot night of the city where killers were on the prowl? I didn't know.

The black coffee scalded down my throat and restored some of my jumbled thoughts to order. Rosemary sat quietly smoking. The man who had killed Schloss had been a stranger. That meant only one thing to me, that the seventh man had completed his job to the point where he could employ professional help. That if I wanted to find the seventh man, my time was running out. I drained the coffee, poured another cup and spied the brown plastic portable radio sitting on top of the quietly whirring electric refrigerator.

I got up from my chair. I didn't want Rosemary to hear, and yet I couldn't keep from turning that radio on. I had to know the damage, and what had been the result of those few minutes in the cellar. The announcer's voice rose smoothly, and when the local news I was waiting for came, every word leaped out from the speaker like a tiny arrow.

"Police are searching for Harry Diamond, newspaper columnist, a suspect in the double slaying of Otto Schloss, Chicago racketeering figure, and an unknown man, earlier this evening in the basement of Diamond's Lakeside apartment. Diamond was seen at the scene of the crime by Otis Paulson, janitor of the building, who said he heard shots and took the elevator to the basement to investigate. . . ."

I turned slowly to look at Rosemary. Her eyes were large in quiet horror. I jerked my head back toward the radio, listening to the effortless syllables weaving an invisible hangnoose in the air.

"Paulson reported having found Diamond crouched over the body of Schloss just outside the service elevator door in the basement. Diamond had a gun in his hand, and Paulson said that when he stepped from the elevator Diamond turned and fled to the alley. Further identification was provided by a key chain found clutched in Schloss' hand, evidently torn from Diamond's belt. On the chain was a key of a professional journalism fraternity. Engraved on the back of the key were the initials, H.D."

I pawed at my belt, seeing the broken belt loop and the circle of tiny gold links still hanging. The chain had broken just below the fastening catch. I ripped the circle of chain loose and stuffed it in my pocket, a tight feeling in my throat. The announcer kept on.

"A city-wide search is being conducted for Diamond, and police are confident that he will be found before morning. We'll have more Chicagoland news after this word from the brewers of Pixley's Beer. . . ." I snapped the radio off with a vicious twist and faced Rosemary.

"You killed Schloss?" she whispered, unbelieving.

I shook my head. "I shot the other one, the gunman. He killed Schloss."

"Gunman!" Fear was soft in her voice. She rose

from the table and came to me, her hands cool on my cheeks, the soft warm scent of her refreshing in the hot night. "Is—this more of the Asperito thing?" she asked.

"I'm afraid so. It's the windup."

"What are you going to do? Turn yourself over to the police?"

I twisted away from her and threw open the kitchen door. I walked out on the dark porch and lit a cigarette. "How can I do that? Paulson identified me as the man who killed Schloss. Even with things like ballistics tests, by the time I got free it would be too late."

"To late for what?"

"To get the leader of the syndicate in this town!" I said softly, facing her, my fists tight at my sides. "To get him for good." I stared up at the sky. An idea formed in my mind, taking shape as each moment passed. My watch showed that I only had a few hours left. In daylight they'd find me. I knew the direction I had to take now. Rosemary stood framed in the kitchen doorway, but I had to shut out the alluring thought of her. The wheel was turning fast. I had a free ride only until it stopped.

The seventh man's hired gunman was dead, but the seventh man wouldn't know whether or not Schloss had revealed his identity. Not only the police would be wanting me now.

CHAPTER XIII

I realized I couldn't stay at Rosemary's.

I started back through the kitchen door. She blocked my way and I saw that she didn't intend to move. Tiny jeweled tears glittered in the corners of her eyes, trembling there, but they did not fall. I stood close to her, gazing down into her upturned face, seeing fear and apprehension there. With a clumsy choking sound I put my arms around her and buried my face in the fragrant warmth of her hair. I let the dry wordless sobs come tearing from my throat until they died away.

"I'm scared," I said into the scented darkness.

"Harry, Harry," she whispered, and I felt her hands on my neck. I hugged her as tight as I could, touching the wonderful human bulkiness of the robe, holding her as something good and right. Her hands moved on my neck and I felt her lips on my cheek, murmuring silently. The rain hissed black beyond the porch. I could feel the dampness of her tears on my skin.

At last I pushed her away and twisted my fingers through my hair. "I've got to get out of here," I said, walking into the kitchen.

She closed the back door and locked it quickly,

coming around in front of me. "Harry, please let me help you."

I started to shake my head, then changed my mind. "Okay. Look. The janitor, Paulson, knows my car. First thing, the cops'll start tracing it. You can let me borrow yours."

"All right, Harry," she said, opening the kitchen door. "I'll drive you wherever you're going." She started determinedly through the darkened front room. I took a step into the darkness.

"*No!*" I said. "I don't want you mixed up in this any more than you are now."

"I'm going, Harry," she said softly. I turned out the light in the kitchen and stumbled my way to a chair. To argue with her now would only waste time. And besides, the thought that she wanted to help me so much boosted my clobbered morale as much as it could be boosted. I heard no movement in the darkness. She waited for my answer.

To compromise, I said, "All right, you can drive me. When we get where I'm going you'll come right back here, though. Promise me that."

"I promise," she said.

"Then hurry." I sunk deep into the chair and lit a cigarette as the light flicked on in her bedroom. She began pulling frothy underthings from her bureau, which was right in line with the door. Off came the robe, then the shorty pajamas that made her look like a little girl. I saw the lithe young body, somehow richer and fuller for the fact that she had fulfilled herself by bearing Tommy. She drew on underthings. I watched, not embarrassed, feeling that there could never be embarrassment between us, almost as if we belonged together, man and wife sharing the companionship of one another without the stupidities of false modesty. I wished to God in that moment we did belong together.

Rosemary turned and smiled gently toward the winking eye of the cigarette, almost as if she had remembered for the first time that I was not a husband. Quickly then, as if she remembered modesty but was too proud to bow to it and ashamed of the fact all in one, she finished dressing. She emerged from the bedroom in a thin cotton house dress, a scarf tied around her hair. She still wore no lipstick. I got out of the chair wearily as she crossed to the door and opened it.

"You want to say good-by to Tommy?" I asked.

She was already in the hall, shaking her head. "He sleeps soundly. I'll be right back." Her car, a blue Ford two-door of the previous year, stood parked a couple of slots down from the apartment entrance. Rosemary slid under the wheel and had the motor going in a moment. "Where to?" she asked.

"Straight up to Wilmette."

Effortlessly she turned the wheel and slid the car down the shining wet pavement. We cruised down the neon strip of Howard Street and made the big turn along the lake into Evanston. The streets lay deserted, most of the lights darkened in the apartment houses.

I slid my hand into my pocket, felt Charlie Parnell's gun and took my hand away again. Whether or not my idea would work was blind chance. If it didn't I might as well lie down and never give a damn again. Rosemary drove faster now, the tires slithering along the pavement. We swung past the Northwestern campus under the great arches of trees and Rosemary put on a burst of speed. We made the first light on yellow, but Sheridan Road was deserted and Rosemary ran the next two reds. After a while the glittering cat's eyes that outlined the name Wilmette on the roadside signboard flashed by. "Slow down," I said to Rosemary. She slowed the car and I reached across and punched out the lights. I saw the home of William Dwight looming in the next block. "Stop," I said softly to Rosemary. She applied the brake and the Ford slid in to the curb. The rain hammered mutedly on the metal roof. I heard the distant rushing of the lake.

My throat tight again, I reached out to pat Rosemary's hand where it was fastened in a tight grip around the steering wheel. "So . . ." My voice faltered. "So long, Rosemary. You take the car home now, promise."

"I promise," she repeated. "Harry—will you call me?"

"Sure I will," I said.

I levered down the door handle. I hesitated, then started to slide out.

"Harry, kiss me. Please."

I kissed her for one quick moment, a moist brush of lips against lips and I didn't want it to stop. But I wanted the seventh man more. I touched her hand again, as if it had magic in it, and crawled out of the car. I slid into the shadow of a high spiked iron fence as she made a U-turn and turned on her car lights. In the glow from a street light I thought I saw her wave but I couldn't be sure. The tail lights fused and then disappeared altogether in the black distance. I started along the pavement, paused at the gate to Dwight's home and stole across the lawn as quietly as I could. Beyond the house a light burned in the garage apartment of Alex Noonan. I made it to the front porch. This is the place to start, Harry, I thought. Go ahead. Get him. . . .

The door was locked. Cursing silently I tried the handle a couple more times. Wiping my sweated palm on my trousers, hoping the noise wouldn't summon Dwight, I thumbed the bell. I pressed back into the shadows and waited, licking salty sweat off my lips. "Who's there?" a reedy feminine voice asked after a moment. My breath sounded windstorm—loud in my own ears. The question was repeated and then I heard a latch sliding off. The door opened and Helen put her head outside. I chopped my fist down on her jaw, and caught her as she fell.

I dragged her inside, lowered her onto the floor, then I closed the door and made my way through the darkened entrance hall. A crack of light oozed out under the study door. I stopped breathing and noiselessly turned the handle. The door opened without a sound, as any rich man's door should open. I stepped onto the patterned carpet. In the deep chair before the dead eye of the television screen, Dwight was immersed in a book, the lamp throwing light on his shoulders that was the only light in the room.

With my gun in my left hand I started forward. He heard something and looked around, his mouth opening for a startled exclamation. My hand shot forward and closed on his throat. I knelt beside him and let him stare at the black bore of the revolver.

"Yell and I'll kill you, Dwight. I mean it." Sweat beaded his powdered skin. He managed to nod his head and I released him. The book dropped with a soft thud to the carpet. I walked backwards, holding the gun on him, and shut the door.

"I heard about your killing Schloss on the radio," he said, wiping a hand down his cheek. The air conditioning had cooled me considerably, but Dwight's face was sweaty.

"Your wife is gone, Dwight," I said. "She left you because she was afraid the seventh man would topple you off the throne, too."

"You're lying," he exploded, rising from the chair. The tanned cheeks seemed to sag. "Who do you mean, the seventh man?"

I explained. "I want him, Dwight. I want the seventh man. And if you want to stay on top, help me get him." He stared at me as if shocked out of his complacent pattern of thought. He took a handkerchief from his dressing gown pocket and wiped his cheeks.

"All right," he said. "I'll listen to you. But—may I have a drink?"

I slid my hand up the wall and flicked the switch. The lights came on.

Dwight removed his black-rimmed glasses and folded them shut with a flat clicking sound. I moved over slowly and perched on one corner of the long polished table. Still aiming the revolver just above the waist of his dressing gown I dug a match from my pocket and then a cigarette. My eyes flicked down for a moment while I applied the flame, and when I looked at Dwight again, he had not moved. It struck me that he had been far less concerned about his wife's disappearance than about his own safety. My dislike of him grew. I laid the paper book match on the surface of the table as the black charred head snapped free. Dwight stared at the wispy curl of smoke rising from the table and winced as if he felt pain.

"Well?" he blurted suddenly.

"You don't need a drink until we talk," I said.

With a small sigh of disgust, he lowered himself onto the arm of the occasional chair. "Just what is it you want me to do for you, Mr. Diamond?"

"I want you to get on the telephone and call Milo Heinz and Jake Bushnell. Tell them both that you're holding me here, a prisoner." Comprehension flitted behind his eyelids. "That's right," I said. "One of those two is the syndicate representative, the man I've been calling the seventh man. When you tell them I'm here, one of them will come, intending to kill me."

"Do you mind telling me why you're so sure of that?" Dwight asked.

"Never mind," I said. A smile ghosted across Dwight's drooping lips, a smile I could not understand. Dwight lifted both sun-tanned hands, palms raised, in an expert bit of play acting. His mouth curled in private mirth. His head bobbed once as a short laugh came from his throat.

"Mr. Diamond," he said smoothly, "how can you be sure that I'm not the seventh man?"

"I can't be sure," I said quietly.

The corners of Dwight's mouth lifted slightly in

satisfaction. He started to speak, thought better of it and remained silent. But the small satisfied smile did not change. I stood up. Dwight watched me from under hooded lids. My left hand balled into a fist as I walked toward Dwight and halted a pace in front of him. I turned the revolver around and extended it to him, butt first. I watched every line in his face, ready for him.

"If you're the seventh man," I said softly, "take this gun. Try to kill me."

Mockery danced in the corners of his mouth. His eyes flicked over the gun and I thought he was tensing himself, preparing to move. His shoulders lifted a fraction of an inch. My arm extended with the gun suddenly felt leaden. Then he shook his head. The stiffness left me and I stepped back one step. Dwight rose and stabbed his hands deep into the pockets of his robe.

"Mr. Diamond," he said, as if explaining an arithmetic problem to a stupid pupil, "I'm not the seventh man. Now I'd like a drink, if you please."

I wiped my sleeve across my mouth, getting rid of the droplets of sweat. I resumed my perch on the table, one leg hanging, and said, "Go ahead." Dwight inclined his head in thanks and moved down toward the desk. Something in his manner indicated that he felt he had complete control of the situation, and it angered me to realize it. I came off the table and darted around in front of him.

"Wait a minute," I said.

"The liquor is in my desk," Dwight said with a helpless sigh.

"Then I'll watch you pour." He went around the

left side of the desk, I went around the right. Kneeling, he pulled open a panel in the desk next to the floor, moved the door all the way back and stood aside. I saw nothing in there but a few glasses, a soda siphon and a fifth. I nodded and he drew out the fifth, a glass and the siphon. He poured two fingers of the liquor, squirted soda down the side of the glass and drank.

"Care for one?" he asked.

"No. Get on the phone and call Heinz and Bushnell." The thought that time slipped by faster than I wanted it to filled every fiber of my body. Dwight took another long pull on his drink and lowered himself into the swivel chair. He picked up the phone, depressed a small red button below the dial, then inserted a brown finger in the dial and whirled it. The diamond on his fourth finger made a fiery circle as his hand followed the dial.

Dwight's eyes lifted impassively to mine for a moment as he waited with the phone cradled against his jaw. Finally he said, "Milo? Bill Dwight. I've got someone here you might be interested in. Harry Diamond. That's right. Oh, he's safe enough. Yes, I've got him tied up," Dwight said in a sudden burst of inspiration. "Yes, I know the police want him for killing Otto."

I moved around to where Dwight could see me. "That's enough," I hissed. "Break it off." He ended the conversation, and put the receiver down heavily.

"I think this is pretty stupid, Mr. Diamond, if you want my opinion."

"I don't. Call Bushnell."

His conversation with Bushnell was essentially the

same. When he finished he said, "What can you possibly hope to gain? Suppose Milo or Jake does show up? What will you do?"

"Take him to the police for the murder of Al Asperito and Otto Schloss."

Dwight shrugged, lifted his glass for inspection. "Mind if I freshen the drink?" I shook my head. The soda squirted loudly and he leaned back in the chair, the glass resting against the belted waist of his robe. "I suppose all we have to do now is wait," he said, and drank.

"You seem pretty damned nonchalant about the whole thing," I said savagely. "If the police get the seventh man you're in a position to stay on top. It ought to be a hell of a lot more important to you than it is."

Again the damnable secret smile floated across his lips. He lifted an index finger and shook it at me. "Suppose . . ." He paused in thought. "Suppose the seventh man does show up—which I doubt since the phone calls I made were so obviously foolish. A man as smart as this seventh man wouldn't be idiot enough to walk into what easily might be a trap."

"He wants me," I said. "I'm gambling on that."

"Why should he want you?" The words were almost barbed insults.

"Because he thinks I know who he is!" My voice had risen to a harsh pitch.

He swirled the liquor in his glass and studied the tiny whirlpool it made. He set the glass on the green blotter and laced his fingers over his belly, leaning far back in the reclining chair, the picture of unworried comfort.

"It might interest you to know," he said, "that I'm now working with the syndicate." The private smile came again, and now I understood it.

I felt as if I had been clubbed. "You're lying," I said to him.

"As you wish." The carelessness of the reply showed he didn't give a damn whether I believed him or not, and I knew then that what he said was the truth. The book-lined walls seemed to tip, ready to topple over the next moment and bury me. The air of the room burned. The muscles in my body, tight-drawn a moment before, loosened.

"If you're working with the syndicate," I said after a moment, "then you know——"

Dwight shook his maned head. "No, Diamond, I don't," he interrupted. "A man named Silver, in Miami, has been my only contact with the syndicate. I made all my arrangements through him." Dwight raised himself erect again. "I don't know the identity of your seventh man, and what's more, I don't care to know." His flurry of motion caught me unready. A sudden, jagged tearing sound came and then the muzzle of a flat black automatic stared at me, clutched in Dwight's tanned fist. "Drop your gun," he ordered. "I mean it. Now."

The revolver hung in my hand. I dropped it onto the edge of the desk as I saw the white strips of adhesive still stuck to one side of Dwight's automatic. "I keep this taped to the side of my liquor cabinet," he said smoothly. "But I'm not such a fool that I'd go for it while you stood over me, Diamond. Nor am I fool enough to take your gun when you're obviously ready for me to do just that. Back up!" he ordered harshly, rising. "Over to the table and sit in a chair."

I stumbled backward, cursing myself for the blunder. Dwight had waited until just the right moment, then released his psychological bombshell so that I would be too surprised to make a move. I sat collapsed in the chair. "What happens now?" I asked.

Dwight drank from his glass. His eyes never left mine. "I'm turning you over to the police for the murder of Otto Schloss."

wight lifted the phone. I sat through an intermin-
le minute until I noticed that he had not depressed
e red button as he had done when calling Heinz
d Bushnell. Dwight cupped the receiver under his
in, holding the automatic in tight to his body, the
uzzle pointed at my head.

"Alex?" Dwight said softly into the phone. "Come
to the study and bring your pistol. Yes, right away."
he phone clicked decisively down on the pronged
adle. "*Now* would you like a drink, Mr. Diamond?"

"No," I said. The only escape from the room lay
rough the door to the hall, far up the room. My
atch indicated a few minutes past two in the morn-
g. Dawn lay not four hours away.

Dwight sat down in his chair again, keeping the
itomatic aimed at my forehead. "I reinstated Alex,"
: told me. "Since I've come around to working with
e syndicate, I feel that Alex did nothing wrong
hen he turned out the lights that night." Nothing
rong? It was the chauffeur who had set the murder
igine loose. By his act he had enabled the seventh
an to play his first card.

"I think we should have Alex in here to watch you
:fore I call the police," Dwight said, his complete

control of the situation mirrored in his offhand ma
ner. "I wouldn't want you to make any attempt
get away. Definitely you belong to the police."

"Dwight, are you the seventh man?"

His eyes closed for a moment, the lids sweeping
again. "Would you be alive this moment if I we
Mr. Diamond?"

That stopped me. I wriggled uncomfortably. T
air conditioning had dried my shirt, made it stiff a
papery. The door opened behind me and I heard Al
Noonan's rough voice. "Something wrong, M
Dwight?" He came down toward the desk, dress
in worn loafers, paint-covered jeans and a gray
shirt. He held a large blue-barreled revolver. Whe
he saw me he looked questioningly at Dwight. "T
newspaper guy, huh?"

Dwight nodded. "He's wanted by the police for t
murder of Mr. Schloss, Alex. You keep your gun
him while I make a call."

"Okay," Alex said, backing off toward the opposi
wall. He leaned against a shelf of books and lit a cig
rette deftly with his left hand. The revolver did
waver. Dwight had laid his automatic, strips of a
hesive and all, on the blotter across from Charl
Parnell's gun. I gauged the distance to the desk a
shifted in my chair as Dwight picked up the pho
once more. "Uh-uh," Alex said. I turned toward hi
A thin smile hovered on his lips. "You'd be dead b
fore you made it halfway," he said.

Dwight spoke briefly to the Wilmette police. Whe
he hung up he said, "They'll be here shortly. And
don't think we'll have any other visitors before the
Mr. Diamond. Neither of the two parties I phone

ill show up. Whichever of them is your man—and
don't give a damn which one is, you understand—
ould be smart enough to see the trick for what it
"

I had minutes now; slippery, fast-running minutes.
lex Noonan was obviously bewildered by Dwight's
st recital, I could see that on his face. But he kept
om asking questions. And he never moved an inch
vay from the shelved books, from where he held the
in on me. I couldn't move.

Dwight unfolded his black-rimmed glasses, fitted
em on and began leafing through some papers on
is blotter. I thought rapidly and came up with some-
ing. "Doesn't it bother you that you'll never know
ho killed Asperito, Roblein, and Schloss?"

"You killed Schloss," he said coolly.

"The hell I did."

Thoughtfully Dwight eased the black rims off again
id held them by the ear pieces, swinging them
owly up and down. "No, it doesn't matter one bit.
m in with the syndicate and as the saying goes, I'm
ean. I've committed no murders. If Linda has gone,
ie's no real loss. She told me she would be out very
ite this evening, at a club, but what you say might
ery well fit in with her character. You see, Dia-
iond, nothing matters very much to me except my
wn health. I'm not stubborn enough to fight the
yndicate and wind up dead. I'd rather retire from
ctive work and take a smaller percentage. I have
nough money to live as I'm living for the rest of my
fe. I value health, Diamond. I'm unwilling to throw
 away because of pride or stubbornness or any other
>-called virtue. You see," and here he tapped the re-

folded glasses gently against the breast pocket of h
expensive robe, "I'm only looking out for the welfa:
of Bill Dwight. Nothing else has any meaning." D:
contempt etched his lips. "Or could a crusader •
the fourth estate understand that?"

I had a slim, dangerous plan now.

"You rotten, low-down skunk!" I said betwee
tight teeth. "You self-centered son of a——"

Noonan swung his gun in a short menacing ar
"You shut up," he cut in. Dwight frowned, u:
certain as to what to make of my behavior. I let ¿
with a batch of obscenities directed at Dwight, spi
ting them out as fast and as vengefully as I coul
Alex Noonan took another step forward. "You qu
talking like that, damn you!" he shouted.

For perhaps another ten seconds I swore, easi:
up out of my chair. Alex sputtered and lowered h
jaw, bulling his way toward me across the room wit
blood-anger in his eyes. Too late understandir
dawned in Dwight's face and he went for the tape
automatic, crying out, "Stay away from him, Ale:
damn you, *stay away!*" But Alex was almost on top •
me now, cursing me in return, not hearing Dwigh
I came up fully out of the chair as Alex whipped th
revolver down in a sloping arc aimed at my head. H
lips worked furiously, his cheeks had darkened, an
he was bent on quieting me and showing his loyalt
to his employer.

Alex partially blocked Dwight from my sight.
slugged the chauffeur in the solar plexus with m
right fist as hard as I could. Saliva flew from Noonan
lips as he let out a rush of air between his teeth. M
left arm caught his below the elbow and blocked th

hopping arc. I clamped my left hand over his right
and slid my finger over his in the trigger guard. He
offered no resistance in that one pain-blinded moment and I pushed his arm out straight and pressured
his finger. The revolver boomed flatly and Dwight
dropped behind his desk. I twisted the revolver out
of Alex's hand and with my hand locked on the barrel, I whipped him on the nose and forehead. He
dropped to one knee, red pulp squirting from his
nostrils down over his upper lip.

Breathing fast I made it to the desk, scooped up
Charlie Parnell's revolver and thrust it into my
pocket. Dwight's automatic still lay on the blotter
where he had not had time to pick it up. I threw it
hard into a corner as Dwight braced his hands on the
edge of the desk and pulled himself back up. I
hopped the revolver across his nose and the blow
made him stagger back against the wall with a moan.

As I headed for the door Alex Noonan came to
his feet. Hissing for breath through clamped jaws
he collided against me and slipped his arms around
me, locking hands in the small of my back. He jerked
convulsively and a lance of pain shot up my back.
Swinging hard with my right hand holding the revolver I hit him on the left temple and he released
his grip. I threw my right arm from left to right with
all the force I had and there was a splatting noise as
the metal slammed across his face. He stepped back,
his palm to his blood-stained mouth, and his left leg
buckled under him. Flailing clumsily he went down
again.

Dwight stumbled around the desk, but I already
had thrown the study doors open and I was running

for the front hall. I didn't stop to notice whethe
Helen still lay there. From the study I heard Dwigh
shouting, "Get up, Alex, get up and go after him!'
Hot sticky rain washed over me as I ran across th
yard to the drive. Planning each move in second
now, with no opportunity to back track if any failed
I angled along the drive toward the garage at th
rear of the house. The doors came open and the finne
fenders of a black Lincoln reflected distant ligh
from the street. I ducked out of the garage again an
up the stairs into Noonan's apartment. On a littere
dresser I found an ignition key after a minute's fum
bling and went down the stairs again two at a time.
slammed the Lincoln's door and rammed the ke
home, hearing the motor ripple softly into singin
life a moment later. I backed out and slewed th
wheel wildly, feeling the tires sink into damp earth
Panic caught in my throat as the rear tires spun i
the muddy earth for an instant. Then the car rocke
forward and started rolling down the drive.

The tires slid and I finally got the car on the cente
of the drive. I pulled past the rear of the house, gair
ing speed, as a figure ran out across the front law
toward the drive. I yanked the lights and saw Ale
Noonan in the blaze, revolver raised, his face a blood
wash beyond the rain-smeared glass. He ran into th
middle of the drive and fired twice, straight at th
windshield.

One of the pair of shots starred the right quarte
of the windshield. Shards of broken glass stung m
cheek. The Lincoln tires whined as I swung the whee
to the right, a trick that had been played upon m

esh in my mind. Noonan's face ballooned larger out
f the darkness, a patchwork of blood stains, and he
irew his hands up before his face. The tires dug the
iwn and Noonan seemed to leap backwards, disap-
earing beyond the rain-filled beams of the head-
ghts. I vaguely saw him crawling away across the
rass as I heaved the wheel left and used the car's mo-
ientum for the pull out of the adhesive earth back
nto the drive. The Lincoln spurted out of the drive
nd the tires bansheed as I headed south, glancing
p only a moment later with a sigh of relief to realize
iat no other cars had been coming.

The darkened trees still showered rain on the wind-
iield, so I kept the wipers at their steady clicking.
Vhere Sheridan turned left in Evanston, I continued
raight on Chicago Avenue, south through red light
fter red light, past the dead glass panes of silent
iops. I knew I had very little time now. The bricks
f Chicago Avenue rumbled under the tires, and al-
iost past the cemetery I S-curved under the railroad
racks. Slewing the car into the curb, I parked it,
alked the long block to Howard Street, and reached
ie grimy El station. A sleepy woman raked my
ossed coins, and I slammed through the double doors
nd went up the steps two at a time. I broke out onto
he platform just as the doors of a two-car train hissed
losed. I slammed both fists on the car door, and a
eedy old man in a worn Transit Authority uniform
eeked blearily out into the rain. I yelled for him to
pen up and a moment later the door hissed again.
stepped inside the empty coach as the train lurched
orward.

I turned and stared out the window at the pattern

of black apartments moving past, dappled here and
there by solitary lit windows smeared around the
edges by the falling rain. I took a deep breath. Safe
for a time. I planned the next move. I got up and
stood leaning against the side of the vestibule, staring out into the rainy darkness. I could walk it back
to Rosemary's from the next station, I decided, and
from there I could start again. My watch showed a
little more than three hours until dawn.

I had a cigarette going when the train rattled to a
stop. I ran down the steps and out of the station, hurrying north at a fast walk. The street lights swayed in
a faint breeze, creaking softly. My shoes clacked hol-
lowly on the sidewalk.

What did I know?

Well, I felt fairly certain that William Dwight was
not the seventh man. He *would* have killed me, had
he been. By murder's process of elimination, that left
two of the original six, Heinz and Bushnell. It took
my mind a minute to recall the day in Tocca's office
when he showed me his chart and enumerated alibis,
but as the incidents came floating back through wall
of tiredness, I thought that Heinz had been one of
the suspects without a proveable alibi. Bushnell of
course had Rita Ray. Short of going to both of them
and pushing a gun barrel down their throats, I had
no way of singling out the seventh man. And then I
remembered that they would be alerted, certainly
by Dwight's phone call. That had definitely been a
mistake. Okay, Diamond, stop thinking of mistakes,
I told myself. The gambling room stays open only until six in the morning.

I had the seventh man, but I had nothing more

than a phantom, a shadow form with a staring oval blank for a face, a killer whose gun hand was gloved, *loup garou* of murder who changed to the human form of Heinz-Bushnell, and behind whose wall of flesh the truth lay crouched and savage, unwilling to be torn loose from the secret womb. *My God,* I thought, *there's absolutely no place to go!* Odds were stacked against me that I could ever get close enough to either of them to beat the truth free.

Could Tocca sweat them? No, not unless he had conclusive evidence, for I knew the refusal to answer on grounds of self-incrimination, the legal evasions of smooth blue-cheeked men with brief cases who could thumb their noses at the blind lady with the scales. The day of third degree had gone, and this was the syndicate, business-like, emerging the victor with infinite patience from the slimy bog of legal obscurities, of time-wasting questions and cross-questions. Tocca would never get an indictment, not with Quinn sitting in the D.A.'s chair.

The night folded dark and hot and futile around me. The seventh man, who had shot Asperito and wiggled out of my hands, who had booked passage for Roy Roblein and given him a vacation without an end, who had sent a hired workman to gun down old Otto Schloss before he talked. Heinz-Bushnell. But *how?* I frowned as I walked, Tocca's face bursting every other second in my mind like a distant sky-rocket in explosion. Tocca spoke to me without words and I knew I should remember something about this night of nightmares. *What* should I remember? I yawned and shook my head. I tried but nothing came.

Rosemary's street lay deserted, rain-slick sidewalk and pavement alive with writhing golden patterns of light. I walked faster. Maybe with one more cup of coffee my brain would come alive again and I could remember what I felt I *should* remember. I hurried along, close to the sheer rising faces of the apartments. Rosemary's Ford stood where it had been parked before. I walked up, using the handrail to pull myself.

When I stepped into the hall every thought was cut out of my mind. I saw a shaft of light thrown on the hall carpet by Rosemary's inch-open door. And the brazen bells of trouble went wild inside me as I raced down the corridor. I tore Charlie Parnell's gun out of my pocket, flattening against the wall. From the other side of the open door I heard ragged, thin, sobbing. I stepped inside. The living room lights blazed. I almost started to laugh when I saw Tommy standing in the middle of the room, wearing blue-and-white-striped pajamas. Then I saw that his cheeks were raw with tears. He recognized me and brushed at his eyes. He sniffed. "They—they took her, they took mommy," he said.

A sickness went through me. I knelt down and took hold of his shaking shoulders. "Who took her, Tommy? *Who* took your mother?"

"Men," he sobbed.

"Who were they? What did they look like? How many, Tommy? Can you remember?"

He nodded. "Three, and they were big. She didn't want to go but one of them hit her. I didn't want her to go, Mr.——" He tried to remember my name but a fresh sobbing made him close his eyes. "I didn't want her to go because they hit her." I felt his small-boy bones trembling under my hands, and I felt defeat. The seventh man overlooked nothing. As Tocca had said, there was nothing they would not do. The seventh man had to know whether or not Schloss had told me too much. The information system of the syndicate had doubtless supplied him with data about Rosemary long ago, at the beginning of the whole affair. They knew how to get to every single person.

"Tommy," I said as softly as I could, "how long ago were they here?"

"I don't know. Somebody's been calling on the telephone. I didn't answer it. I thought mommy might come back." He collapsed against me then, digging his small fists into my back, bewilderment choking out in each of his sobs. I held him and stared into the room. *My* fault. They had taken Rosemary. Tommy turned his head to look at me. "Mr.—Mr. Diamond," he said, remembering, "where did they take her? When's she going to come back?"

"I don't know, Tommy," I said. "I don't know."

"I want her to come home," he cried in the unreasonableness of fear. "They hit her! Why won't she come home?"

"We'll get her home, Tommy," I said, not knowing how, trapped. "Sure. We'll get her. . . ."

From the bedroom, loud as death, I heard the sound of the ringing telephone.

CHAPTER XV

I stood up. The phone died in silence. Tommy's rounded eyes looked up at me questioningly. He sniffed again and rubbed a hand across his right cheek. "Tommy," I said intently, "if I promise to try to get your mother to come home, will you do something for me?" He nodded as the phone shrilled to life again, sounding more insistent. "You go out into the kitchen and get a glass of milk or something. I'll come out in a minute. Will you do that?" The phone cut off again, the echo of it hanging in the air.

"Okay," Tommy said, his voice barely above a whisper. He turned and shuffled toward the kitchen in his bright red bedroom slippers. I waited numbly, watching until he reached up and snapped on the kitchen light. The phone aroused itself with another demanding ring. I walked rapidly into the bedroom and quietly closed the door behind me. With a sweating hand I lifted the receiver from the small table standing against the wall.

"Hello," I said.

"Diamond?" Immediately I tried to place the voice; the voice that was thickly disguised in some way, nearly indistinguishable. Behind the man

speaking I caught sounds of movement, another
voice lifted in a clipped syllable. I had the receiver
jammed tightly against my ear, listening for every
detectable sound.

"This is Harry Diamond," I said.

"Guess who this is." I heard a flat cold snicker from
the background.

"I can't."

"I hear you call me the seventh man." The voice
waited for an answer. I had nothing to say. My eyes
roamed the bedroom, the frill-shaded lamp on the
night table, the tangle of underthings on the seat before the dresser, a collection of lipstick tubes that
shone with flat gold highlights. The room smelled
fresh and clean, every inch of air breathing with the
life of Rosemary. "I've got some instructions for
you," the seventh man said.

"Go ahead," I said.

"I'm holding the woman," the voice said. "I want
you to wait where you are, in her apartment, until
I get there. If you don't wait, I'll kill her." A sound
came over the wire like a snapping of fingers and the
voice spoke to someone else, muffled, more distant.
"Bring her over here." Sounds of movement, a sudden rush of quick breathing. "You talk to him," the
voice said.

Rosemary's voice: *"Harry, get out of there! Take
Tommy, and——"* The thick slap of flesh striking
flesh sounded flatly across the distance and I heard a
low sob from Rosemary. Another voice told her to
shut up and there was a pause, accompanied by more
of the sounds of movement.

"You see," came the voice of the seventh man again, "I've really got her. One of you is going to die, Diamond. It's up to you which one." He paused again. "Are you listening?"

"Yes."

"You just can't keep running, and you might as well get that straight. Bill Dwight called my man Silver after you left. I figured sooner or later you'd turn up at the woman's place, with the cops after you. I've got to get rid of you, Diamond; you've stuck your nose in too far. Maybe you haven't figured out who I am, but I give you credit. You would after a while. I don't think the cops will. They haven't dug like you've dug. . . . Diamond?" he said then, punching out the word explosively.

"I'm here."

"Good. You stay there. I'll be over right away, and if you're not there, I'll pick up that phone you're talking over and call my boys. When I call them, the woman gets killed. Clear?"

"Yes."

"Good." The voice chuckled. "It's going to be quite a surprise for you, seeing me. Or have you got it figured out which one of the six put that note on the table?" A slight difference in tone came into the voice, as if the seventh man was not as sure of this part as he had been of the rest. I took the receiver in my right hand and moved the fingers of my left to get rid of the tension.

But now I knew. I had been told, clearly and definitely, earlier tonight; and now I remembered. *I knew.*

"No," I lied. "I haven't figured it out."

"Well. You will. Remember, stay right there, or the woman gets killed. Clear?" he repeated.

"Clear." With a final click the connection died.

A sound behind me made me whirl. Tommy had pushed open the bedroom door, and he gazed up at me. A pale milk mustache filmed his upper lip. "You said you were coming out."

"I—I had to talk to someone on the telephone."

"Was it mommy?" he asked, faint hope lighting his eyes.

"No, but it was somebody who told me where I could find your mother. Tommy, go get some clothes on and we'll go find her. Okay?"

"S-sure," he replied shakily. A small sad smile crossed his lips, and then he bolted from the door and I heard his running steps retreat toward his own room. I shook a cigarette from my pack, walked over and sat down on the bed. *No time,* I thought suddenly. I walked back to the phone, working calmly now because I had no seconds to waste. I knew who the seventh man was, but could I get to him in time? His thick stupid face lied, his cheap ill-fitting clothes lied, his whole appearance lied, hiding a deadly mind behind a small-time, dull-witted front.

Could I find Rosemary before Jake Bushnell had her killed?

I picked up the receiver and dialed Artie Roth's number. A sleepy female voice answered. "Let me speak to Artie, please. It's urgent." Urgent? She didn't know how urgent.

"Wait a minute," the woman mumbled. "I'll call

him." From another part of the apartment came the only sound I could hear, a drawer being torn open. Tommy was hurrying, at least. I deliberately kept thoughts of failure out of my mind. Great as the chance of failure loomed, dwelling on it might only insure its happening. The receiver rattled as it was lifted at the other end and Artie's sleep-dazed voice said, "Hello."

"This is Harry. Listen. Can you get a car? I mean right now?"

"Sure, boss," Artie answered, bewilderment in his voice. "I can get the old man's."

"Then get it." I gave him a place to meet me on Lincoln Park West, near Clark. "What kind of car is it?"

"Green Dodge fifty-one sedan."

"Listen, Artie, for God's sake don't waste any time. Don't even bother to get dressed. You've got to be there when I get there. Rosemary's in trouble."

"Okay, boss, I'll——"

I slammed the phone down and left the bedroom. I stabbed out a half-smoked cigarette, and hurried into Tommy's bedroom. He was pulling on a Space Cadet sweat shirt, and his voice came out from under the cloth, muffled. "I'm all ready, Mr. Diamond." The sweat shirt slipped down over his neck and he ducked into the closet, emerging with a green jacket. He had on blue jeans and only the red slippers on his feet. Well, he had no time for shoes now.

"Come on," I said.

He followed me doggedly into the bedroom. A search of the dresser top proved useless. Desperately

I ransacked the rest of the room, then started on the front room. Thrown carelessly down on the cushion of one of the easy chairs was Rosemary's purse. I managed to get it open and found the keys to the Ford inside. Tommy and I left the apartment without turning off any of the lights. Tommy's tears had been replaced by an eager grin, and he bolted ahead of me down the stairs. Happiness had come back into his world now that we were going to find his mother.

If he knew, I thought. . . . I couldn't look at my watch.

I could only hope the time would hold out. Because if I did not pull this off, if I was not somewhere at the precise moment, all the hands on all the watches in the world could not make a difference. I U-turned the Ford on screaming wheels and roared for Sheridan. Tommy sat alertly with his legs dangling over the edge of the seat. The light went yellow as I approached the street and I skidded around the corner without slowing.

"I'm going to leave you with a friend of mine, Tommy," I said, talking low and patiently to him. He protested and I said, "I can't take you to where your mother is." No, not when I didn't know myself where she was. "But I promise you if you go with this friend of mine and be a good boy, I'll do everything I can to bring her home. Is that okay?"

"Sure," he said cheerfully. "Anything you say."

I thanked God that he did not understand, could see none of the darkness in my words, none of the close precious shaving of seconds. Foster Avenue came up ahead and I skidded left and onto the Outer

Drive, the speedometer needle moving inexorably around the dial, fifty, fifty-five, sixty, and Tommy smiled the clean smile of hope beside me.

Artie's green Dodge stood parked on Lincoln Park West, under the rising cliff face of the Parkway Hotel. I got out of the car, circled the Ford's hood and levered down the door handle for Tommy to crawl out. I took his hand inside mine and led him up to the sidewalk door of the Dodge. Artie leaned across to open the door for us, the round bowl of his pipe glowing for a moment. The light crawled up his face and died. I let Tommy slide in the front seat and then I followed him, my feet hanging out on the pavement as I breathed the air thick with the greenish smell of the park.

"Artie, this is Tommy, Rosemary's boy. Take him home with you and look after him." Artie's eyes met mine grimly in the next sudden burning of his pipe. He nodded and twisted the ignition key, starting the motor. I slid quickly back out of the car. "Artie's a good guy," I said to the boy. "You'll have a lot of fun at his house."

"Tell mommy where I am," he reminded me.

"Sure." I forced a grin as I pushed the door shut and stepped away. Tommy's face pressed against the glass as he waved. The Dodge slid quietly around the corner toward Clark and I ran back for the Ford. The game had high stakes now, and if I lost the next throw I'd be out of the game for good. I put the thought of Tommy's face and his wave from my mind as I gunned the Ford south. I cut into the park, tunneling under the thick curtain of trees, and took

Dearborn going south. At a cross street I went left, finding a slot two doors from the apartment I wanted. Rain pattered down again as I walked back and hurried up the stone stoop into the musty humidity of the old building. A bulb in a brown paper shade dangled on each landing, shedding forlorn light on the frayed carpet. The second floor apartment vibrated with the brittle sounds of a party. Two at a time I mounted the next steps, Charlie Parnell's gun weighing securely in my fist. Light showed from under Rita Ray's door as I rapped demandingly. I waited. Footsteps slithered across a carpet and halted beyond the door. The lock rattled, and then, as if she thought better of it, she asked, "Yes?"

"Open up, Miss Ray. It's Harry Diamond."

I listened carefully but heard no sudden catch of breath. Not everyone in the city could have heard of Schloss' death, I reasoned. The door opened perhaps two inches, and Rita Ray stared out at me, her face without its make-up an ugly landscape of whitish blotched skin. The turban bound her russet hair once more, and blue silk pajamas hung loosely from her shoulders. The pajama sleeves ended below the shoulder, and in the haze of diffused light from behind her I saw that she had no freckles on her arms. The skin was pitted along the vein path with red needle punctures.

Apprehension lay on her face but before she could speak I thrust the revolver forward through the gap, twisting the pajama material with the barrel. "You'd better open up," I said. "I'm not kidding." Her eyes flooded with quick terror and then she pushed the door forward half an inch, threw the safety bar back and pulled the door wide. I stepped inside quickly and used the sole of my foot to jam the door shut again. An expression of false composure crossed her face as she knotted her hands together.

"What do you want?" she asked. The darkness of her eyes, invisible in our former interview, now leaped out at me, the pupil centers round with artificial dilation. A disc jockey's drone floated out of the console behind her. She saw that I stared at her eyes and she hastily lowered her eyelids, the breathing sounding in a dry whisper through her nostrils.

Now the fragments of the picture puzzle began to drop out of an invisible sky and fall into place on the board. "Where does your friend Jake Bushnell hang out, Miss Ray?" I said.

With fast returning self-consciousness she folded her arms, using her spread fingers as best she could to conceal the needle marks. She turned away from me, shoulder blades thrusting out like knives under the blue shimmering material of the pajamas. "Why do you want to know?"

My left hand fastened on her right shoulder and I dug my fingers in, turning her around. I held tight while I pushed the revolver muzzle into her chest below her breasts. My voice was harsh from more than the long night of nerve-wearing exhaustion. "I told you I wasn't kidding. Where is Jake's office? If I have to beat it out of you, I guess I can." The eyelids flicked down again like closing blinds. "Look at me!" I said. The dilated pupils became unhooded. "You know I'm not kidding."

"Okay," she said. "Jake's office is the Knockout Gym on Madison."

"The address?"

She gave me an address near the Stadium. I slipped my hand down to tighten on her right wrist as I put the revolver into my pocket. I hated to spend the time in doing what I planned now, but on the other hand I thought that death for Rosemary could be only a step away if Rita Ray lifted the telephone and dialed the Knockout Gym.

"What are you going to do?" she asked, her voice edged with panic.

"Tie you up." I pushed her ahead of me. With a little snarl she jerked her arm up and tore loose. The savage protective instinct glittered in her empty eyes as she dove for a low bookcase, her sharp scarlet nails closing around a heavy metal bookend. I ducked in low as she swung, my left hand catching her wrist again and my right palm smashing her along the jaw. Her head snapped and the bookend fell, thudding heavily on the rug. I gave her the other hand along the jaw, breath hissing between my teeth. She put both hands to her head, pressing her temples in a dazed manner. I pushed her ahead of me into the small cubbyhole bedroom and sat her down on a dresser bench. Her head bowed, she seemed to be gazing helplessly at the angry red ruin of her arms. With the revolver in my left fist aimed in her general direction I pulled the top sheet loose from her bed. I stretched her on the floor and bound her ankles, then pulled up the bottom sheet and bound her arms to her body. The handkerchief from my rear pocket went wadded into her mouth. I flicked out the dresser lamp and closed the door on the darkened room, hearing a clumsy thrashing behind me. Another small

chair slipped under the door knob and I left the
apartment, having already wasted precious minutes.

How long would it take the seventh man? Perhaps
his car had already slid to a stop before Rosemary's
apartment. Perhaps he had already opened the door
and found deserted emptiness. I drove west on Chicago Avenue and south on Halstead, too wound up
now even to put a cigarette in my mouth. The Ford
shivered and rattled over holes in the pavement.
Street lights shone at irregular intervals in the deso-
late wasteland of warehouses and truck terminals
here beyond the river. The night wind streamed in
through the open windows, washing me with hot
rainy moisture. Neons sprouted along the sidewalks
now, and in a few moments I made a right turn onto
Madison, driving down between the noisy haunted
walls of this canyon of despair. The colored lights
threw a changing pattern of brilliance over the car's
interior. Flashes of juke music blared and died, a
sharp female voice wailing about love in a sudden
burst of sound, only to be lost a moment later behind
other sounds. I cut around a streetcar and slid from
lane to lane, forcing the brake down once when I
saw a motorcycle cop parked at an intersection. The
Ford leaped forward again and the blocks stretched
out. . . .

The bars had ceased to cluster one next to the other
in endless procession. The buildings became older,
darker, used-car showrooms set next to used furniture shops. I began searching for street numbers. I
slowed the Ford and a Yellow cab spurted around
me, tail lights dwindling fast. Traffic died out here.

The Stadium bulked with square solidity against the red smears of the rainy sky. Then I saw the sign, hanging out over the sidewalk, unlit bulbs surrounding the painted name: "Knockout Gym."

CHAPTER XVI

The entrance was a narrow door set between two darkened shops. I slipped inside and started up the steep stairs, moving fast but moving with care to be quiet. The very walls gave off an ingrained stench of human sweat that grew more powerful as I climbed. The stairs ended in a narrow landing, with an inner door whose dark window blind was drawn. I turned the knob, gave the door a gentle push and it swung open perhaps three inches. Beyond, darkness. I drew out Charlie Parnell's revolver and slid through, my back flat against a wall. Light filtered through the ropes of a ring in the center of the lofty room, and as my eyes got used to the black, I saw what appeared to be an office, my view blocked partially by the ring itself. Ducking low I circled the ring on the right and knelt at its corner. From there I could see the office.

The office door stood open, and there was a large oblong window next to it. A thick-faced man in a blue pin-stripe suit, maroon shirt and black tie sat in a chair tilted against the wall, staring dully at the end of his cigar. In the center of the office, before a littered desk, Rosemary slumped in another chair, her eyes closed. The sleeves of the housedress had been ripped. Even from the distance I could see the polka-dot pattern of reddish blotches on her upper arms. Why they had done it, burned her, I did not know. I crouched, animal-like, next to the reeking canvas and felt the hatred of them scorch like a white flame.

On the office desk, the telephone rang.

I came up out of the crouch, knowing who waited on the other end of the wire. From the part of the office I could not see appeared a short, wiry man wearing a Panama hat. The man against the wall jerked forward and his chair hit the floor loudly. The smaller man said, "I'll get it," and reached for the phone. By that time I had started my walk forward, and I brought the revolver up and squeezed the trigger just as the smaller man's hand cupped downward for the receiver. The crash echoed through the gym. The cigar dropped from the hand of the other man who ripped his coat open and tugged at the heavy automatic stuck into the band of his trousers. I shot once more and the reaching hand of the smaller man sprung open like a trap. He turned toward me on corkscrew legs and fell forward, but I caught sight of the torn holes in the belly of his white shirt before he struck the floor.

The other man swept his hand down the wall and the lights blinked out in the office. I backed up a step. A rush of footsteps came from the office door and I jerked the revolver down abruptly. Firing into the darkened office I could hit Rosemary. I took another step backward, listening. I heard urgent breathing, I thought from somewhere to my left. With one hand resting lightly on the ring canvas I started to walk that way. From the opposite side of the ring a gun exploded and I dropped to the floor. I lay with my face against the wood. I waited. The sound of breathing came again, and then footsteps slapped on the canvas ring floor above me. They came toward me cautiously, the shoe soles protesting with the faintest of squeaks.

I doubled my legs under me and came to my feet. I shot once toward the center of the ring and dropped. Two shots answered, and the canvas tore as a third plowed downward into the floor. I crawled two feet to the right, lifted my head over the edge of the ring and fired once more. I dropped back and waited. For a moment of infinite time I thought I had missed. Sweat rolled down my forehead across my cheeks and a drop fell from the point of my jaw. Then I heard it, the weary expiration of breath, and the canvas vibrated as the body struck.

Standing up, I felt for matches in my pocket and found a pack. I laid the gun on the edge of the canvas and raked one of the matches alight, and raised it, peering into the ring. The flame danced on the face of the sprawled man, lighting his helpless, puzzled dead expression. His eyes glared like two opaque marbles. The match burned down to my fingers, stung, and I dropped it. The mask and the marbles vanished.

A sound penetrated my mind then, dull and insistent. The phone had not stopped ringing. I crossed to the office, lit another match and found the wall switch. I went behind the desk, where I could see only Rosemary's slumped back, and a grim sort of satisfaction came over me. The wild note of the phone shattered the office like a desperate scream.

I sat down in the chair, placed the revolver on the blotter where I could see it, and lifted the phone.

"Jackie?" The pitch of the voice had risen a little and each word was audible, probably because it was no longer disguised. "What the hell took you so long to answer?"

"This isn't Jackie," I said. "This is Diamond."

"*Diamond . . . !*" A baffled exclamation.

"Diamond," I repeated. "They're both dead, Bushnell." A sound of a caught breath when I spoke his name.

Then he seemed to get control of himself. "How—how did you find her?"

I thought that one over for a moment. I was still a long way from Jake Bushnell, and so were the police. Finally I said, "Rita Ray told me."

"*Rita* told you? That cheatin' . . ."

I laughed a short laugh. "I think you're through," I said. I slammed the phone down as hard as I could to let him hear the sound of his own failure. Rosemary's head shifted a little and she groaned. I went around the desk and knelt by her, touching her right shoulder gingerly, feeling the injured rawness of her flesh. I took her cheeks between my palms and rubbed them. Her eyelids flickered.

I rubbed her cheeks harder, afraid with an unreasoning fear that the life had gone out of her. The absence of make-up accentuated the drawn paleness of her face, but at last her eyes opened into slits, and behind the lids her eyes drained of tortured weariness. "Harry?" she murmured, not quite believing. She licked her lips and groaned again.

Crawling around behind the chair I worked loose

the knots in the clothesline and lifted her limp hands into her lap. I worked on the raw rope burns of her wrists and when she opened her eyes again they remained open. I tried a grin at her. "Hi," I said, unable to think of formal words. The corners of her lips twitched; her way of smiling. "It's just me," I said.

"Tommy. How's Tommy?" Her eyes opened wider and she strained forward in the chair. "Did they . . . ?"

I pushed her back gently. The stiffness left her neck. "No, no, Tommy's okay. Artie's got him, he's staying at Artie's house, Tommy's fine." The eyelids closed. "Rosemary? *Rosemary?* Can you hear me?"

Her head moved up and down the tiniest part of an inch. "I . . . can hear you, Harry." Her hands lifted, and she held the sides of my jaw gently between her palms. "I hear you. Tommy . . . I was afraid. . . ." She sucked in breath quickly, her right hand moving to her left shoulder. She barely touched the flesh, and moaned again. I got up awkwardly and went to her side, leaning over, holding her and touching her right cheek with my face. I closed my eyes. Rosemary turned her head, eyes closed, and I felt the dry brush of her lips on my cheek.

"I'll get you to a doctor right away, Rosemary," I said. "Can you wait till I make a phone call? To the police?"

"I—I can wait, Harry . . . yes." She dropped her hands in her lap again and breathed deeply. I pulled the phone across the desk, dialed O and while the operator rang police headquarters I put a cigarette in my mouth. The smoke curled up and stung my eyes but I had never tasted a better cigarette. Now I gambled again. Jake Bushnell could retreat, could cross the state line in a matter of an hour or two and perhaps never get caught. But seven words repeated themselves inside the laughing part of my brain, seven words for the seventh man, a kind of irony in that: *"Rita, huh? Rita told you? That cheatin' . . ."*

"Police headquarters," said a clipped male voice.

"Captain Tocca. It's urgent."

"Who's calling?"

"This is Harry Diamond," I said. The soft exclamation of surprise from the other end brought a weary smile to my mouth. On this one night my name could open doors! Several clicks rattled along the wire.

"Captain Tocca speaking." He sounded tired, too. "Diamond? Where the hell are you? If you don't come in you're liable to have a murder tag on you, you know that? Why the hell did you run?" He sounded sore.

"Shut up, Captain. Listen: Do you want the seventh man?"

Tocca's voice was savage. I knew what this meant to him. "Diamond, if you start kidding me now, I'll fix it so you never——"

"This is the truth," I cut in deliberately. "The seventh man is Jake Bushnell. And don't ask now why I know. If you want to catch him trying to kill somebody, get over to Rita Ray's apartment." I gave the address. "I don't know for sure if he'll turn up there, but I think he will. Better cover the roads, the stations and airport in case he tries to run. But get to Rita Ray's apartment. I'll meet you there right away."

There was a moment of silence. I knew that Tocca was discouraged; through his mind would run thoughts of failure, of this being impossible, of a hook somewhere, that the end couldn't come this way, not when he had labored so long and run against wall after unbreakable wall. "Rita Ray's apartment," he said, his voice carefully controlled to keep excitement out of it. "Okay. I'll be there. And I hope for your sake that you are, too."

He broke the connection before I had a chance to answer.

CHAPTER XVII

I climbed out of my jacket, and at the end of a few painful moments Rosemary was on her feet, swaying weakly. She could not lift her arms herself so I helped her into the jacket and buttoned the three buttons. She trembled, and my arm around her middle kept her from falling. With one short anguished step after another we worked our way to the stairs. Then I preceded her down, walking backward with my hands on her waist, lifting her from one step to the next. Her hand slid along the rail and as we reached the street I saw that the backs of the knuckles shone white and bleached. She shook her head and collapsed at the last step. I caught her, staggered, then hooked my free arm under her legs and carried her. The air had cooled slightly with the coming of the deepest hour of night. I carried her across the street and put her gently on the front seat of the car. She folded forward with a sigh, legs doubled under her, hands pressed against the cushions and face pressed upon her hands like a Moslem in prayer. Soundlessly then she slid over on her side, curled up. I felt her back, panicked; at last I detected the faint rhythmic rising and falling of her breathing.

Heading east on Madison, the lights blurred and

blended into a pattern of speed. I drove steadily with a wash of cooler air fanning my face. In exactly sixteen minutes I crossed Dearborn. Traffic and the life of the town died at this hour. Street lamps retreated, lonely yellow sentinels ranged down the blocks. I slowed to a stop at the intersection and searched the darkness. In the shadows of a building two men lounged, so still that they blended perfectly into the murk around them, and I only saw them because I had looked hard. I left the car angled in the middle of the intersection and got out. I walked rapidly to the sidewalk and one of the shadows slid out to meet me. A fountain-pen shape gleamed dully for an instant and then vanished.

"Is Captain Tocca up the street?" I asked.

"Yeah," the cop answered.

"I'm Harry Diamond. He's looking for me."

"You can get up to the apartment building if you keep in the street lights as you go. We got men who know Jake Bushnell."

I pointed to the car. "There's a woman in there who needs medical attention, and right away. Can one of you take her to a hospital?" The shadow swiveled toward its companion, who said nothing. "Look, I'm not kidding," I said. "Bushnell hurt her and she needs a doctor. I'll tell Tocca, but that woman needs help."

"Okay," he said. "I'll take her." He pocketed his gun and without a word threaded his way between bumpers of parked cars. The Ford's door closed, the gears gnashed for an instant, and with a rising hum of power it disappeared down the street to the south. I took another long breath.

"Bushnell hasn't shown yet?" I said.

"No," came the toneless voice from near the wall. "We got the block covered tight."

"I'm going on up to the building."

"Okay." I thought for a minute that I might have been talking to a phantom. They were all around, hidden in the shadows. At the corner I turned to stare back, but my eyes made out nothing except the solid sheet of darkness where the building met the sidewalk. I walked fast, and I couldn't keep from probing into the inkiness of porches and areaways for a sign of them. I saw no sign.

When I opened the street door and stepped into the lower hall, the air lay deadened and empty, yet filled with presences. I knew that Bushnell would find nothing wrong. They had hidden perfectly, and still they were there, shapes with guns standing so still, hidden beneath the stairs, that I could hear the sound of their lives ticking away the seconds. I went up the stairs and the sounds of the party had died on the second floor, and they were there too; I sensed them, but I never saw them. I passed through the pool of light on the third-floor landing and knocked gently on Rita Ray's door.

The door opened and a gun barrel nosed out. I heard a sound behind me. A man stood caught in the light pool now, shadow black, except for the out-thrust cylinder of gun metal and the yellow brilliance of his Panama crown and brim.

"Come on in, Diamond," the voice beyond the door said. The man on the landing melted back out of the light. I stepped into the black apartment. The man next to me said, "Captain Tocca is sitting on the sofa inside. Go on in."

I worked my brain hard to capture a plan for the apartment, and with that in mind I inched my way slowly toward the couch. Abruptly I stepped on someone's toe. He said nothing. I backed off hastily and lowered myself onto the sofa. A spring gave a tiny pinging protest which the buttery stillness smothered.

"He hasn't shown yet, Captain?" I whispered.

"No," Tocca whispered back. "If you've got a gun. . . ."

"I get the first shots," I said.

"Listen . . ." Tocca raged softly.

"*You* listen. He tried to kill me." I thought of Rosemary. "He's mine."

A pause. Tocca's sigh. "All right."

I loosened Charlie Parnell's revolver from my pocket and held it in my lap. We talked only in whispers. My eyes made out an oblong faintly smudged with red across the ceiling. "You think he might come through the skylight?" I asked.

"He might come any way," Tocca replied. "What I want to know is why you feel so sure he's going to come. I won't pass this up, Diamond. Not on your life, not even if he's out of the state by now. But you think he'll show up here?"

"I do." Suddenly a thought bolted through my mind. "The Ray woman. Did she . . . ?"

"We've got her tied up on the second floor," Tocca said patiently. "She's on the stuff, if anybody ever was. You tell me why Bushnell will be here."

In the passing seconds I sketched in the long trail

of my nightmarish wanderings since Schloss first phoned me at my apartment. "I told Bushnell that Rita Ray had tipped me off to where he was keeping Rosemary. He sounded mad enough to kill her when I talked to him over the phone the last time. I took a chance that he'd come back here and try to do it. He must have known that I'd call the police and that he'd have a hard time trying to make it back here. I figured if he got desperate enough, he might get personal, too."

Tocca grunted. I could not see his face, but I felt that he must be frowning doubtfully, there in the dark beside me. "Tell me how you figured it out to be Bushnell," he said at last. I could hear the wounded defeat coming from his lips now, and I took it easy.

"You remember when I told you about Schloss dying? I asked him who the seventh man was, and all he kept muttering was *'Fear, fear.'* He said it over and over. I couldn't make any sense out of it. Then later on I remembered that when Schloss got excited he suddenly lapsed into German. You know any German, Captain?" He grunted negative. "Well, I don't know any either, but I've seen a couple of those comic German bands, you know, where the leader stamps his foot to start, and counts, *'Eins, zwei, drei . . .'* After three comes *vier,* and when I first heard it, I thought Schloss was pronouncing our English word *fear.* He wasn't. It was *four.* Before he died his mind went off on a crazy tangent, I guess, and he could only think of one thing. The chart you showed all the suspects that day in your office. Jake Bushnell was number four on the chart, number four around the table, and Schloss remembered that, and he told me in German." I stopped, then said, "If he hadn't remembered anything, we wouldn't have had a prayer."

I waited tense for a strained moment, and then from Tocca came, "That crazy chart did it, huh?"

"Yes."

The sound that came, another grunt, might have expressed some degree of pleasurable satisfaction. I hoped so.

"The alibi was fixed, of course," I said. "And there's a good reason for it. Rita Ray took dope, and Bushnell supplied her. The first time I saw her, in dim light, I thought she had freckles on her arms. They were needle marks. No wonder she'd lie for him."

"We found the punctures all right," Tocca replied. His voice harshened in its whisper. "Damn it, if that Quinn hadn't clamped down after the first questioning. . . ."

"Captain," I said, "if you get him, you'll get him without Quinn's help. That'll be better, won't it?"

He actually chuckled then. "Earlier tonight, Diamond, I thought you were a pretty stupid guy. I was wrong."

Was he? The minutes dragged and the apartment and the world still lay dead quiet. Tocca began to shift more often, wriggling from side to side and breathing more heavily. Sweat broke out under my shirt and on my palms. I was sure now that I had made this last gamble and had gambled wrong. Bushnell would never come. Bushnell was out of the state. Bushnell . . .

The silence shattered with a sound of breaking glass. My head whipped up. Crouched like some crooked demon against the sky, a man's shape bulked beyond the skylight as he hacked at the glass with the barrel of a revolver. I came up off the sofa, holding Charlie Parnell's gun. Bits of broken glass rained in a tinkling shower on the carpet as the man over the skylight chopped again to widen the opening. He grunted as if every blow dealt against the panes was freighted with hate. Tocca eased himself from the sofa to stand beside me. Sweat streamed down my forehead. Towering, the man on the roof reared back and jumped. His feet crunched down on glass when he landed in the room.

CHAPTER XVIII

Bushnell moved away from us, walking heavily. It was apparent that he knew his way around the apartment, since he made for the bedroom door and kicked it open. I heard the voice that had come over the phone twice in the last few hours, a voice that cajoled softly into the darkness, near to pleading, but somehow holding undertones of cruel anticipation. "Rita? Wake up, Rita . . ."

The footsteps retreated into her bedroom. A light snapped on and I saw Tocca's face for the first time in the illumination. The heavy brows thrust forward and down in concentration. The automatic in his hand had a flat menacing look. From the vestibule came another man, carrying a gun. Tocca warned him off by shoving his gun barrel down. Bushnell appeared beyond the doorway, gargling in wrath. He ripped back one of the bedsheets and flung it on the floor.

"Bushnell," I said.

The seventh man whirled, his face seeming to fall to pieces, his hair disheveled, the bulky green plastic raincoat he wore slithering as he turned. His mouth snapped open as he jammed his revolver against his hip and fired, teeth rigidly clamped, his mouth working

ng. I shouldered Tocca out of the way and slipped to
one knee. Bushnell's shot missed me. I fired the instant afterward, three times, feeling hatred boil, ex-
plode like a bomb and wash away the moment the
echo of my shot died. An acrid odor drifted across
the room. The other cop took a step forward, ready.
Bushnell's face worked itself into a maudlin expression of sorrow, near to tears.

"Oh, God!" he said.

He fell against the door frame, clutching at it for
support. His right arm under the raincoat grew black.
For a moment his hollow eyes stared out at us. I
thought I saw them gleam with shrewdness, as if the
syndicate agent's brain lodged behind the face that
acted and tricked you had suddenly come up with
salvation. Then the gleam died. His gun thudded
hard on the wooden floor. The other cop picked it up.
I dropped Charlie Parnell's revolver back in my
pocket. The room became crowded then as the silent
watchers from the hall came through the door. Tocca
made his way through the knot of men and had
sense enough to turn on a pair of small table lamps.

I sat back down on the sofa. I could have killed
Bushnell, yes. But I had my own reasons not to. For
now the police had him alive. And he would know, in
some bitter stone-walled cell, that he couldn't write
off Harry Diamond with a wax pencil, a target pistol
or a hurtling Cadillac.

I wanted to drag my legs off the floor and go to
sleep without another word. Tocca conferred with
his men and I heard the sound of a phone dial whirling. Tocca pushed his way out of the group and came
toward me. His transparent plastic raincoat was

thrown open, and under it he had on a pair of crease
less sun tans and a blue sports shirt, worn with tai
outside his belt and decorated with yellow flowers
He looked more like the proprietor of a Florida
motel than a Chicago cop, but that was all right, too
None of us were what we seemed. Rita Ray never
had freckles, Jake Bushnell did not appear from the
outside to be a syndicate organizer, and Harry Dia
mond, when revenge was finished, was only a man
who wanted sleep.

Tocca smiled down at me. "Go on home and hi
the sack. Come into the office when you wake up and
you can make a statement. I don't think there'll be
any trouble over that Schloss business. Bushnell's
broken." Tocca shook his head thoughtfully. "When
they go to pieces, they go all the way. You never saw
a man so shot, Diamond. Listen." I listened and from
beyond the wall of backs where the detectives clus
tered came a hoarse hiccuping sob.

"It's like he's finding out for the first time that he
can lose," Tocca said. He surveyed his own detectives
over his shoulder. "The slob!" he said with utter dis
gust.

I stood up. "I didn't want to kill him."

Tocca snorted. "He wishes you had, I'll bet. No
he'll live." With a balled fist he tapped me lightly on
the shoulder. "You go on home now. I've got to stick
around for the doc." He rubbed a sweaty hand under
his nose, scrubbing his lips with his palm. The wed
ding band winked gold. "When I wind this up, hell,
I'll sleep for a week." Without further word he
turned and pushed his way into the press of men. I
waited another minute, then left the apartment.

The rain had started again, hotter than ever. Between the buildings a soiled gray light smudged the sky in the east. I yawned once or twice, too tired to lift my arm for a look at my watch. I let my shoulders sag as I fished a cigarette out of my pocket.

I trudged all the way to the Clark and Division subway station. Then I waited twenty minutes for a train and walked the seeming miles to Lakeside. I was even too exhausted to wonder a great deal about Rosemary. She'd be all right in the hospital. I just about made it to the bed in my apartment. Limp gray light spilled from the lake and slanted obliquely into the room, growing a paler gray by the moment. I had no dreams.

I woke up around three-thirty, cooked a breakfast and phoned the Broadway garage. The attendant retrieved my car from near Rosemary's and it was worth the five dollar bill for him to stop in front of the apartment and honk. I drove down the Outer Drive through curling tendrils of muggy mist and went to Tocca's office. I filled out the statement and we talked until quarter to six. Then we had a steak and a beer at a grill down the street and talked more.

Tocca ran his tongue around the rim of his glass, collecting foam. "The syndicate's all done here for a while, Harry." The use of the first name pleased me somehow. "The doc patched Bushnell up and he started talking. We've got enough to indict Milo Heinz, too. *And* a list of names!" His palm slapped the table, and he seemed filled with almost boyish exuberance. "My God, we'll scour out every rat's hole in Chicago before we're done."

"What about Quinn?" I asked, forking my last bite of steak.

"When your paper and the others increase the pressure, Quinn'll move or he'll be through. My guess is he'll try to welsh and the office'll be vacant. I think we can drum up somebody who'll do a real job. Golly, how O'Riordan would have loved this." A frown knitted his brow. "Hey, that reminds me. I promised you a story, but your paper got it this morning along with the others. One of my men handled the release. I'm sorry, Harry. I was so damned bushed I didn't think. . . ."

"I don't want the story," I said with feeling.

. We left the grill and I walked back to police headquarters. Tocca stood on the sidewalk while I started the Chevvy. He had his hat pulled low to fend off the slanting rain, but I had ceased caring about the weather. Tocca had told me that Rosemary would be well and out of the hospital in a day or two, though she would need a fairly long rest.

"I could never get sore at you for butting in," Tocca told me with weary humor. "You wrapped the whole thing up for us, and I'm sort of ashamed. But I wouldn't trade the outcome for anything."

"I didn't mean to wrap it up for you," I said. "Not last night. I was worried about Rosemary mostly, toward the end."

Tocca's eyebrows lifted as did his shoulders. "Maybe that's why you did a good job, huh?" He bent and extended his hand through the open window. "Listen, drop in and see me from time to time."

We shook, the pressure hard and firm. "I will, Captain. Thanks."

"So long." His wave was jaunty and he turned, walking up the three steps and into headquarters building, the raincoat falling cleanly away from the proud lift of his shoulders.

Days later, I sat on the edge of Rosemary's bed. A temporary break in the weather had brought a clear blue afternoon sky, and the curtains on the window belled under the pushings of the crisp lake breeze. The apartment had the smell of fresh air in it, mingled with the fresh scrubbed aroma of Rosemary's skin. A glow of health had come into her cheeks again, and she wore pink lipstick. Her back was propped against the headboard, a pillow under her shoulders.

Tommy was at school. Neither one of us had spoken of the night when so much had happened. I felt that, regrettably, whatever closeness we had known had been a product of the fear and the peril bred by the night. I had not seen the photo of Joe McClennen anywhere in the apartment. I wondered if Rosemary had put it away.

Rosemary studied me for a moment, a half-smile forming on her lips. She put her hands in mine and without preamble said, "Harry, I love you so."

I kissed her then, her arms locked behind my head, and it brought memory back of the desperate kiss that night near Dwight's home. Here was a wonderful woman, lovely, rich in body and in mind, and I wanted her. Her lips brushed against my ear. "Harry, I'm well now. I—I don't care if you don't ever want to marry me. . . ."

I moved back gently away from her. "What's

wrong, Harry?" she asked. I looked away. She touched my hand.

"I'm sorry," I said. "I'm a nut, that's all. I can't explain it." Her eyes darkened, hurt. "Look here," I said hurriedly, "I don't want you to feel that way. You're the finest woman in the world, and nobody knows it better than I do."

"What is it, then? Joe?"

I nodded. "Partly, I guess." I studied her closely. "You still love him a little, don't you? It's no crime to be in love with two people, Rosemary. And I know you didn't mean that about no marriage. If it's ever going to be, that's the only way." I stood up, trying to grin brashly and not having much luck at it. "I suppose I've just got one hell of an inferiority complex, that's all. There's nothing to be so sad about. I'll come around before long. But one thing sure: I've learned to appreciate a certain amount of mothering."

The conversation ended there, but I was grateful that the hurt look had vanished. I kissed her good-by lightly and left. In the sun I walked up the block to where I had parked my car. Diamond, you boob, I thought, you're just plain stubborn. You have to be the big guy all the time. I opened the car door and rolled down the windows. The freshly washed hood shone with metallic highlights. The air smelled lake-fresh and sweet. I had work to do at the paper.

I drove back past Rosemary's building and glanced briefly up at the window, her window. I wanted her but I had to work on my own bollixed brain for a while, one part inferiority, one part stubbornness, and one part—which I hated to admit—plain orneriness which bolted at the bogey-fear of being tied down. The seventh man was finished, but now I had Rosemary and *that* I wanted to work on. Plus the column to get going again, really going at the old semi-efficiency, and *that* I wanted to work on, too.

The sun splintered off the hood as I cruised down the Outer Drive. The lake threw white foam at the rocks and two kids played on the grass with a harlequin-colored plastic ball. The river that's been called time, or history, or life, keeps on going and one problem melts into another problem and that in turn remelts, and the river pushes on. Things will work out. I believe that.

More Best-selling
Espionage and Suspense
from Pinnacle Books

GET ACQUAINTED!
THREE BESTSELLING
ACTION/ADVENTURE SERIES
FROM PINNACLE BOOKS